Ice Cream and Incidents

A
Peridale Cafe
MYSTERY

AGATHA FROST

For questions and comments about this book, please contact
pinktreepublishing@gmail.com

www.pinktreepublishing.com
www.agathafrost.com

Edited by Keri Lierman and Karen Sellers

ISBN: 9781983190049
Imprint: Independently published

ALSO BY AGATHA FROST

The Scarlet Cove Series
Dead in the Water
Castle on the Hill
Stroke of Death

The Peridale Café Series
Pancakes and Corpses
Lemonade and Lies
Doughnuts and Deception
Chocolate Cake and Chaos
Shortbread and Sorrow
Espresso and Evil
Macarons and Mayhem
Fruit Cake and Fear
Birthday Cake and Bodies
Gingerbread and Ghosts
Cupcakes and Casualties
Blueberry Muffins and Misfortune
Ice Cream and Incidents

A

Peridale Cafe

MYSTERY

Book Thirteen

CHAPTER 1

The annual Peridale fête landed on a beautifully hot day in the middle of May. After a miserable start to spring, Julia South was happy to feel the sun on her skin as she stood behind her cake stall in the grounds of St. Peter's Church. She had baked a large batch of lemon drizzle cupcakes decorated with intricate flowers made of icing to celebrate the village being in bloom once again. Most of the cakes had already sold, so she was glad when she spotted Jessie hurrying across the village green with a fresh batch.

"These are quite delicious," said Father David Green, the vicar of the church, "and very pretty indeed! You've outdone yourself again, Julia. Your wonderful baking always raises a generous sum for the cause, and I'm sure the unfortunate homeless individuals we're trying to help will be very grateful for your support." David took another bite of his cake as Jessie approached the table, the lemon buttercream sticking to his upper lip. "And here's the young woman of the hour!" he exclaimed when Jessie shuffled past him. "Julia, you must be incredibly proud of your daughter for helping to raise awareness for such a worthy cause."

Jessie smiled meekly, her cheeks flushing with embarrassment as she set out the fresh cupcakes on the display stands. With Jessie's eighteenth birthday weeks away, Julia was extremely proud of her foster daughter's growth. Not only because she had lived on the streets before Julia had taken her in, but because her social conscience and recent fund-raising efforts had led Father David to pick a local homeless shelter as the recipient of the money raised by the fête.

"I am very proud," Julia said as she watched Jessie sink further into her baggy black hoody. "Not many people her age have the empathy to want to help people less fortunate than themselves."

"Indeed," Father David muttered through another mouthful as he fished a pound coin from his leather wallet. "I'll take another if you don't mind. So very delicious."

After picking up a second cupcake, Father David joined the long line in front of Barker's stall in the shadow of a large oak tree. It had been a month since Julia's fiancé had shot to national fame thanks to the release of his debut crime novel, *The Girl in the Basement*, but Julia had yet to grow used to his new local celebrity status. Barker had swapped his role as the local detective inspector for full-time author life, and even though Julia had been apprehensive about him retiring from his police career, the beaming grin on his face as he signed books at his stall told her he had made the right decision. She had even had an influx of tourists visiting her café with copies of Barker's book in the hope he would be around to sign them, which he usually was, thanks to him working there while writing his second novel.

"Have you heard from Kim yet?" Jessie asked, her tone anxious as she buried her hands in the pockets of her hoody. "It's my birthday soon."

Julia shook her head, Jessie's nerves echoing inside her. She had been calling Jessie's eccentric social worker, Kim Drinkwater, multiple times a day, but Kim had stopped answering her calls and had yet to reply to any of Julia's frantic voice messages. With Jessie's eighteenth birthday so close, they were both growing suspicious that the promised adoption would not be finalised in time.

"Kim promised it would go through," Julia said, trying to push forward a reassuring smile so as to not make Jessie worry even more. "She said it was as good as official."

"Kim's word doesn't mean a thing," Jessie huffed with a roll of her eyes. "Until I see the documents saying that you and Barker are my legal parents, I'm not going to rest."

"It *will* happen."

"Kim has let me down before."

"And this won't be one of those times," Julia said, cupping Jessie's soft cheek in her palm. "I called social services this morning, and they said they were going to chase it up. Have faith, Jessie."

Jessie nodded that she would, even if her face showed something different. With her head low, she walked across the church grounds to her brother, Alfie, who was looking through a stall of second-hand books. Julia did not blame Jessie for being sceptical about the adoption. After being separated from her brother at just three months old, and then spending sixteen years in the care system, Julia was sure it would make even the toughest cookie cynical.

As was always the case with the spring fête, every resident had come out to enjoy the stalls and the beautiful weather. There was something for everyone, from Julia's cakes and Barker's books to tarot readings from Evelyn and Father David's homemade jam. Julia's father, Brian, and his wife, Katie, arrived a little before noon with a wallpaper-pasting table and half a dozen brown boxes. They set up next to Julia's stall, and before she could ask what they were trying to sell, Katie ripped open one of the boxes to reveal bottles of 'Glow Like Katie' fake tan.

"We've not had any luck getting them into the shops yet," Katie said with a girlish giggle as she set the bottles up on the table after spreading out a bright pink sheet. "Might as well put them to use for a good cause."

Katie, who was the same age as Julia, had what most people would call a '*fake*' aesthetic. Her peroxide blonde hair contrasted starkly with her bottle-bronzed skin. Her face was caked with exaggerated makeup, and her outfits were usually tight and revealing, even though she had only given birth to Julia's baby brother, Vinnie, six months ago. Despite the initial friction that had arisen when Katie first joined the South family, Julia had grown to love her for who she was. Under the glamorous shell, she was a sweet and caring woman, if not a little child-like sometimes.

"Fake tan?" exclaimed Evelyn, the eccentric owner of the B&B, as she took a break from giving tarot readings. "What an unusual item for the spring fête! How *exciting*! I foresaw a strange object coming into my life with purpose. The tea leaves are *never* wrong. What shade is this?"

"There are three," Katie announced giddily, visibly excited about having her first customer. "Maple, Terracotta, and my personal shade, Walnut, but I refer to that one as the 'Katie Special'."

ICE CREAM AND INCIDENTS

Katie held out her arm, which amazingly resembled the shade of a walnut dresser Julia had in her dining room. Evelyn looked from the bottle to Katie's arms, and to Julia's surprise, she appeared to be considering buying the product despite her own pale skin, which resembled a moon glow rather than a suntan.

"It's just *perfect!*" Evelyn announced as she reached into her yellow kaftan to pull out her purse. "I knew when I stopped looking, I would find the perfect shade! The universe works in mysterious ways."

"You're *not* going to regret it!" Katie said, accepting Evelyn's money. "You're going to look radiant! You'll be 'Glowing Like Katie' in no time."

Katie pulled a sheet of pink stickers from one of the boxes with that very catchphrase printed on them and picked one off to apply it to Evelyn's kaftan.

"*Tan?*" Evelyn chuckled with a shake of her head. "Oh no, dear. This is the perfect shade to stain a wooden table that I saved from a skip! A little colour and polish and it will be as good as new. It's amazing what people throw away these days."

With that, Evelyn moved onto Julia's stall and

bought a cupcake, before returning to her own stall where a small line had gathered for their readings. Katie looked like she was somewhere between confused and offended, but Julia's father appeared amused.

"A *table?*" Katie shrieked, her squeaky voice making Julia wince. "It's for the skin, not a table!"

"But you've just sold your first bottle," Brian said, pecking her on the cheek. "Well done, sweetheart. You'll be selling out in no time! This business venture was a genius idea. You'll see."

Katie looked slightly consoled by Brian's praise, but her enthusiasm was lessened when the next customer came by and left without even picking up a bottle for a closer look.

Leaving her father in charge of her cake stall, Julia decided to explore the other offerings at the fête. She bought a jar of orange marmalade from Father David's stall, a book about Victorian baking from Betty Hunter's, and a knitted teapot cover from Shilpa Patil's. After grabbing two hot dogs from the food truck, Julia wandered over to Barker's table, where the line of people wanting their books signed had yet to relent.

"Ketchup and mustard," Julia said as she handed him the hot dog. "Just as you like it. I thought you'd be hungry."

Without missing a beat, Barker bit into the hot dog, but instead of taking his time to chew, he gobbled the whole thing down in a matter of seconds before licking the sauces from his lips. Malcolm Johnson, the president of the Peridale Green Thumbs gardening society, stared at Barker as though he had just witnessed a dog walking on its hind legs. He passed his book over silently, and Barker scribbled his signature on the inside page after wiping his fingers on his jeans.

"Thanks," Barker said to Julia before accepting the next book. "I didn't realise there were still so many people in Peridale whose books I hadn't signed. I'll be lucky if I can even hold a pen at the end of today."

Leaving him to continue with his work, Julia went in search of her gran, Dot, who she had not seen since the fête had started. As she walked casually around the grounds smiling and waving to people she knew, she spotted Jessie and Alfie sitting on the church wall, both laughing as they ate hot dogs. Not only did they have the same laugh, but they also looked eerily similar. If it was not for the ten-year age gap, Julia might have thought they were twins. It warmed her heart to see them so close after spending seventeen long years estranged.

"Have you seen Dot around?" Julia asked Jessie before smiling and nodding at Alfie, who was wearing a sleeveless grey vest so that his tattooed arms were on show. "She's done one of her usual disappearing acts. She said she'd cover my stall if I needed a break, but I've had to leave my dad in charge."

Julia glanced back at her stall and chuckled when she saw her father wiping sweat from his brow as he counted out Shilpa's change.

"*Huh*?" Jessie said, still laughing as though Julia had just walked into her dream. "Oh, Dot? Yeah. I saw her."

Jessie took a bite of her hot dog and turned back to Alfie as though she had just given Julia useful information. Alfie laughed under his breath before jerking his head at Julia. Jessie licked ketchup from her lips as she looked back at Julia.

"Do you know *where* she is?" Julia asked.

"You only asked if I'd *seen* her."

"Excuse my little sister," Alfie said as he dabbed

at his lips with a napkin, his tattooed hands and arms glowing under the bright sun. "She thinks she's funny. We saw her buy a bunch of raffle tickets from Amy. I think she snuck around the back of the church."

"She looked like she was up to something," Jessie added. "But then again, when isn't she?"

"That is very true," Julia said to herself as she left the siblings to continue talking about whatever they had been before she burst their bubble.

Leaving the hustle and bustle of the fête behind, Julia walked down the dark path between the church and the village hall. She came out at the graveyard behind the church. Wondering what on Earth her gran could be doing back there, Julia wandered past a row of the old, leaning gravestones and scanned the area. She questioned if Dot had ventured into the dense woods at the bottom of the yard, but Julia shook that thought from her mind.

Julia turned to walk back to the path, but she jumped out of her skin when she spotted Dot sitting cross-legged on the grass, her back leaning against the church. She was staring intently at something in her lap, which Julia quickly recognised as Barker's book.

"Dare I ask what you're doing back here?" Julia called, shielding her eyes from the sun as she approached her. "I was about to report you as a missing person."

Dot held up a finger and continued reading until she reached the bottom of the page. Using the dust cover as a bookmark, she closed the book and finally looked up at Julia.

"What was that, dear?" Dot asked as she fiddled with the brooch holding together the stiff collar of her white blouse. "I'm afraid I was lost in your fiancé's book."

"I thought you weren't much of a reader?"

"I'm not," Dot said, her hand resting on the cover of the book. "But this is *rather* good! I got him to sign a copy to sell it on the internet. People are willing to pay *fifty* pounds for signed copies, and fifty pounds is fifty pounds. I merely opened the book to scan the first page to see what all the fuss was about, and before I knew it, I'd finished the first chapter!"

"And you're sitting behind the church because…?"

"I wanted some peace and quiet," Dot said with a wave of her hand as though it should have been obvious. "Billy is at my cottage fixing the toilet, and that lot at the fête sound like a bunch of cackling hyenas. It's hardly the environment to get lost in a work of fiction, is it? Who would have thought Barker would be such a talented writer?"

Julia looked at where Dot was up to, noticing that she was less than a quarter of the way through. She wondered if her gran would think the same way when she reached the sixth chapter, when Dora, an eighty-something year old lady with an affinity for wearing brooches and sticking her nose into other people's business showed up.

Before Julia could forewarn her gran, a megaphone-assisted voice announced that the raffle was about to be drawn. With the energy of a woman half her age, Dot sprang up with no assistance and opened the back cover of the book to reveal five full sheets of raffle tickets.

"How much did they cost?" Julia asked as Dot looped her arm through hers.

"Not a lot," Dot said airily as she dragged Julia towards the path. "The grand prize is a *mystery* holiday! Much better than last year when I only went home with a coupon for your café."

"Not that you ever pay," Julia reminded her.

They emerged from the path and re-joined the fête. Everyone had left their stalls and were gathered around the raffle table, which had been set up in front of the large church doors. Amy Clark, the church organist, was standing on a stool behind the array of prizes, a megaphone in her hand. She adjusted her baby pink cardigan and brushed down the pleats in her powder blue skirt as she waited for everyone to gather.

"I hope you all have your tickets handy," Amy announced, her voice crackling through the megaphone. "The raffle has already raised a record amount, so I'd like to thank everyone who has bought a ticket." Amy glanced over to Dot, who was passing the sheets down to Julia, and nodding for her to pass them on to Barker, Alfie, and Jessie, who had joined them in the crowd. "And I'd also like to thank everyone who has donated prizes. We have a fantastic array of goodies to be won this year, including a holiday!"

An *oooh!* swept across the crowd, and Julia noticed that everyone was holding at least three tickets. Julia looked down at the page she had, which included twenty tickets with all the numbers between forty and sixty printed on them.

"You bought one *hundred* tickets?" Julia whispered to her gran. "You're beyond belief!"

"A *holiday*, Julia!" Dot whispered back out of the corner of her mouth. "Amy has been hyping it up for weeks. I wasn't going to let somebody else win it, was I? It's as good as free."

Father David plucked the first winning ticket from a box and passed it to Amy. She unfolded it before announcing that the winning ticket for a free afternoon tea for two at Julia's café was number thirty-seven.

"That's me!" Dot announced. "I won it!"

Dot carefully detached the winning ticket, but Julia took it from her gran and passed it to the nearest person in the crowd, who just so happened to be Shannon Crump, a barmaid from the local pub.

"That's mine!" Dot cried.

"You can have a free afternoon tea any time you like," Julia reminded her, nodding to Shannon to claim her prize. "And you do, regularly."

Dot huffed but allowed Shannon to keep the ticket. Over the course of the draw, Dot won a toaster, a coffee machine, a free meal at The Comfy Corner restaurant, a free pub lunch at The Plough, coupons for several boutiques on Mulberry Lane, and even a massage at a gym outside the village. When it came time for the grand prize drawing, most people were sending daggers in Dot's direction, not that she seemed to notice. With her remaining tickets clutched in her hand, she looked hopefully at the stage as she waited for the announcement.

"And now for the mystery holiday!" Amy announced, pulling an envelope from the table. "A holiday for four people next weekend! It's quite exciting, and the perfect finale to our fête. Which one of you lucky people is going to win?" Amy glanced awkwardly at Dot, and Julia could tell Amy was praying that someone else won. Father David plucked a ticket from the box and passed it to Amy. After unfolding it, she let out a relieved smile and looked out into the crowd. "Number one hundred and twenty-one!"

Dot looked down at her own tickets, and then Julia's.

"What do they go up to?" Dot asked down to the line. "*Hurry!*"

"One hundred and twenty," Jessie said, holding up the final sheet. "You're one off!"

Dot's eyes darted open, and her jaw slackened. She looked around the crowd, half the eyes staring back at her, and the other half rummaging through their own tickets.

"Oh!" Evelyn exclaimed with a giddy hop. "It's *me*! I won!"

For the first time since the draw had started, there was a smattering of applause. Dot watched as Evelyn pushed through the crowd, her kaftan floating behind her.

"I bet she foresaw that number was going to win!" Dot said as she ripped up her remaining tickets. "Well, that's one hundred pounds down the drain!"

"You spent a hundred quid?" Alfie asked, half laughing, half shocked. "Dot!"

"They were a pound each," Dot replied with a wave of her hand. "And it was for a holiday!"

"*And* a good cause," Jessie added. "And it's not like you're going home empty-handed, is it?"

Julia watched as Amy handed the winning envelope to Evelyn, who had a beaming smile until the white paper touched her fingers. Her expression morphed into something that scared Julia, and for a moment, she wondered if Evelyn had suddenly fallen ill. Nonetheless, she posed for Johnny Watson to take a picture for *The Peridale Post* and retreated to her spot at the back of the crowd.

"Well, that's that," Dot said with a heavy sigh. "At least I'll get some free meals out of it."

The crowd parted, and people returned to their stalls to finish up the last hour of the fête. Julia walked back to her cake stall, and her father looked more than a little relieved to hand back the key for the mini safe. He re-joined Katie behind her tan bottles, not that it seemed like she had sold anything since Evelyn.

"If I'd just bought *one* more ticket!" Dot cried as she plucked a cupcake from Julia's stall without offering to pay for it. "Just *one!* What are the odds?"

But before Dot had even taken a bite out of her cupcake, Evelyn shuffled over, the envelope in her shaking hands, and a grim expression on her face. Julia smiled at her, but Evelyn could barely return it.

"I want you to have this," Evelyn said, forcing the envelope into Dot's hands. "I couldn't go on that holiday in good faith. You wanted it, after all, and I only bought one ticket."

"Evelyn, you don't have to do that," Julia said with a reassuring smile. "You won it."

"I sense something dark within this envelope," Evelyn whispered, as though she was delivering a secret prophecy. "Perhaps it was the spirits telling me that Dot should have won, or they were forewarning me of something else, but it is not in *my* cards to go on that holiday. Please, Dot. Take it. Just be careful. What I felt might not have been solely exclusive to my destiny."

With that, Evelyn turned and hurried away. She quickly packed up her stall before running back across the village green to her B&B.

"You can't keep that," Julia said as she folded her arms. "It's not fair."

"You heard the woman!" Dot cried, a smile returning to her face. "It was *my* destiny to have this, and I don't feel anything dark. In fact, I feel something positively beaming within here. Oh, please let it be a cruise!"

Dot ripped the envelope open and pulled out a sheet of paper, a frenzied look in her eyes as she excitedly unfolded it. It only took reading one line for her excitement to drop.

"Blackpool?" Dot cried, turning to look in Amy's direction, who was packing up the raffle table. "A week for four in Blackpool? That's not a *holiday*! It's not even out of the country!"

"Blackpool is nice," Katie offered meekly. "They have the tower, and the circus, and Madame Tussauds wax museum, and the sea, and the piers, and the rollercoasters, and the -,"

"*British weather*!" Dot interrupted. "No wonder Evelyn felt something dark within this envelope. She was sparing herself the disappointment!"

"You'll probably enjoy it," Julia said, trying to conceal her amusement as she watched Dot read the rest of the letter. "A week by the sea will do you a world of good."

Dot considered Julia's words for a moment before folding up the paper and stuffing it back in the envelope.

"Well, it's a week of not using my electricity," Dot said as she tucked the prize into the small handbag where the rest of her vouchers were stored. "And don't look too pleased with yourself, Julia. You're coming with me. You might as well bring your fiancé and Jessie too. There's no point wasting three tickets."

"But I have the café," Julia replied quickly with a shake of her head. "I can't just –"

"I'll look after it!" Katie exclaimed enthusiastically. "We both will, won't we, babe?"

"We will?" Brian replied, looking at Julia unsurely. "If Julia doesn't mind, I suppose."

"She doesn't!" Katie cried, clapping her hands together. "Oh, this will be so much fun! It will finally get me out of that dusty old manor."

"I'm not sure," Julia said, not wanting to hurt Katie's feelings. "It's not as easy as it looks, and there's all the baking."

"I can bake," Brian said confidently. "Your mother taught me a thing or two."

"She did?" Dot and Julia replied in unison, both sharing the same shocked look on their faces.

"Go and have fun in Blackpool," he said with a deep chuckle. "It's only a week. What's the worst that can happen?"

"Oh, I'm a little excited now!" Dot said. "I suppose Blackpool is better than nowhere. I haven't been since my honeymoon in 1952, so I suppose it will have changed quite a bit since then. I'll tell the others."

Before Julia could protest, Dot hurried across to Barker's table, where Jessie and Alfie were standing. She told Jessie and Barker, who both looked over at Julia with the same quizzical expression. She could only offer a shrug.

"You *won't* regret this!" Katie cried as she pulled Julia into a tight hug. "It's going to be so much fun!"

"I guess I'm going to Blackpool," Julia muttered, her face mushed up against Katie's ample chest.

CHAPTER 2

J ulia spent the next week attempting to teach Katie how to run the café, but by the day before they were due to leave, Katie had only just about wrapped her head around the buttons on the till. She had wanted to cancel the whole thing more than once, and the only thing that had stopped her was Katie's unparalleled enthusiasm. Katie had said on more than one occasion how she was excited to have a 'normal'

job for the first time in her life. Most people would have taken offence to such a statement, but Julia understood. Aside from a short-lived stint as a glamour model in her twenties, there had been no reason for Katie to have had to work. With the great Wellington fortune showing no signs of running out soon, the heiress' need for a 'normal' job had never materialised.

Julia woke with the singing birds on Friday morning after a night of restless sleep. She had weaved in and out of dreams that had focussed on her café being destroyed in various ways. As she rubbed the sleep from her eyes, she was sure the last dream had revolved around Katie somehow setting fire to the cakes in the display case and then trying to serve them to customers while still burning.

By the time Julia jumped out of the shower, Barker and Jessie were also awake. A plate of freshly buttered hot toast and a cup of peppermint and liquorice tea greeted her in the kitchen; she was too touched to tell them her stomach was in knots, so she ate it anyway.

Julia tried to say goodbye to Mowgli, but he hid under the bed as though he knew he was being deserted. She wondered if her father would even see Mowgli when he came in to feed him and clean his litter tray. After loading the cases into the back of Julia's vintage aqua blue Ford Anglia, they drove down the winding lane into the village. The weather had remained beautiful since the fête, and there was not a cloud in the morning sky. Julia had checked the forecast for Blackpool, and it seemed the weather there was going to be just as clement, not that the forecast soothed her nerves about leaving her beloved café.

After parking outside Dot's cottage, Julia knocked on the front door after trying the handle. It was locked, but that was usual for Dot, especially recently. She had watched a documentary on 'home invasions' and was sure burglars were coming for her savings tin any day now. When Dot finally answered the door, Julia was taken aback by her gran's appearance.

"Morning, love," Dot said with a croaky voice before dabbing at her nose with a handkerchief. She was still in her nightie and slippers. "I'm afraid I've come down with the dreaded lurgy. I've been up all night coughing and sneezing. You're going to have to go without me."

Dot demonstrated a cough before rubbing her nose again as she stared at Julia without blinking. Julia did not need a degree in detection to see that her gran was lying and probably in tip-top health as usual.

"Lurgy?" Barker echoed. "Isn't that a made-up illness that people use when they want to get out of things?"

"A cold then!" Dot exclaimed, her tone a little too loud. She seemed to catch her break of character, so she dabbed at her nose and hunched over before coughing. "Maybe even the flu. Poor Amy Clark has it too. I saw her in the post office yesterday. She sneezed all over me without covering her mouth. Quite rude! That's how the zombies are going to get us, you know. People don't have the common decency to keep their bugs to themselves these days."

"But you've been talking about nothing else all week," Jessie said, a brow arched as she looked down her nose at Dot. "I thought we were going to have a fun week?"

"I'm sure you will," Dot said quickly, turning to look up the stairs as Alfie walked down with a large bag. "I've convinced Alfie to take my place."

Julia smiled at Alfie, even though a small part of her had been glad that Dot was feigning an illness. She had hoped it would be her perfect opportunity to call things off entirely. She knew there was still time to throw a spanner in the works, but Jessie looked too excited that her brother was coming, even if he seemed less sure to be taking Dot's place.

"You'll need this." Dot handed over the envelope with the voucher inside. "I called the B&B last night, and they're expecting you this afternoon."

"Is something going on?" Julia asked with narrowed eyes. "I feel like you're up to something."

Julia looked past her gran and spotted Barker's book on the side table in the hallway. The dust cover showed Julia that she was three-quarters of the way in. Dot shuffled to the side, blocking her view.

"You're far too suspicious," Dot said as she pushed Alfie over the threshold before closing the door to a crack. "Not everything requires an investigation, dear. *Go*! Have fun! You don't need an old lady cramping your style."

The door closed, and Dot immediately locked it behind her. Julia even heard her slide the chain across as though she thought Julia would try to let herself in with her key.

"She seemed fine last night," Alfie whispered as he slung his bag over his shoulder. "She woke me up at the crack of dawn and told me to pack a bag. I thought she was kicking me out."

Julia stared at the curtain as it twitched. When she met Dot's eyes, the curtains closed again.

"Let's set off," Julia said, turning back to her car with an uneasy feeling about the whole affair. "We don't want to get caught in the afternoon traffic."

DURING THE THREE HOUR DRIVE UP TO Blackpool, Alfie, a keen traveller who had visited most corners of the world, filled them in on the Lancashire coastal town's history. Situated in the North West region of England, Blackpool's popularity as a tourist destination had been cemented by the 1840s when railways connected it to the rest of the country. By the 1880s, the town had three piers and was famous for having bed and breakfasts, fortune tellers, fish and chip shops, theatres, pubs, and donkey rides on the beach, and they were all still there to this day. In 1894, the famous Blackpool Tower was built in the centre of the promenade. Despite never having visited the town, Julia knew about the 500 feet tall iron tower, which was an iconic symbol of Northern England.

"It was modelled after the Eiffel Tower," Alfie said, craning his neck from the back seat to look up at the large structure as they drove slowly along the promenade. "You can see it for miles around."

"It's huge," Jessie said. "I feel dizzy looking at it. Imagine that thing falling over."

"The Victorians planned for that," Alfie said. "It's been designed so that if it were to fall over, it would fall into the sea. It even sways in the wind rather than fighting against it. Just wait until we get to the top."

"To the *t-top?*" Jessie replied. "Are you crazy?"

"You can't go to Blackpool and not visit the top of the tower," Alfie replied with a wink. "It's been there for over a hundred and twenty years. Don't worry. It's perfectly safe."

"I'll take your word for it."

"There's a three storey building at the bottom too," he continued. "That's where the circus and the world-famous Tower Ballroom are."

Julia looked up at the tower, the rust-red iron

structure contrasting brilliantly with the bright blue sky. Like Jessie, she felt dizzy trying to look all the way up. She looked back to the bright pink horse-drawn carriage they were following along the promenade. She had not known what to expect from Blackpool, but she had not expected it to be so busy. They had been crawling along at five miles per hour since reaching the seafront. She was sure she had heard that the tourist town's popularity was in decline, but there were no signs of that as she looked around. The roads were packed with cars, the trams riding up and down in front of the beach appeared full, and she could even see people sunbathing on the long stretch of sand. The pavement in front of the B&Bs and shops to her right was bustling with hundreds of people. The fresh sea salt air drifted in through the rolled down windows, mixing pleasantly with the scent of freshly cooked fish and chips as they passed one of the many chippies they had driven past so far. When she spotted the Central Pier's Ferris wheel, she knew they were nearing their destination.

"It's called Sparkles by the Sea," Julia said as she looked along the row of B&Bs they were approaching. "From the looks of the map, it's quite big."

They all joined in the search for the B&B, their eyes seeming to land on it at the exact same moment. Sparkles stood in the centre of a strip of ordinary B&Bs, but their destination looked anything but ordinary. Bright pink and five times wider than the B&Bs on either side, Sparkles faced out to sea with a vibrancy that was sorely missing from the other drab buildings.

"It's so huge," said Barker.

"It's so pink," Jessie added.

"It's so Blackpool," Alfie said with a grin.

Julia followed the road to the end and turned up a side street for parking as instructed on the map. After scraping together enough coins to cover the parking for the week, they took their bags back to the promenade and walked down to their new home.

Standing on the pavement as people hurried by in either direction, they stared up at the blinking blue neon 'Sparkles by the Sea' sign. A smaller sign underneath advertised it as a 'Cabaret Show Bar Bed and Breakfast', two concepts that needed to be seen to be believed. The left half of the ground floor seemed to house the bar aspect of the business. It had its own entrance and tables outside, all of which were full. Even through the darkened windows, she could tell that the bar was packed with people. The right side of the ground floor appeared to be the hotel's restaurant, with the upper floors occupied by the bedrooms. There were more windows than Julia could count, but the flashing 'NO VACANCIES' sign let her know they had at least won tickets to a popular place.

Bags in hand, they walked silently to the hotel's entrance, which was marked with another neon sign. Julia led the way through the vanity bulb-lined front door and into a small vestibule. Framed pictures of glamorously dressed women covered the walls. It took Julia a moment to realise they were drag queens. The centre picture, which was more significant than the rest, advertised a beautiful queen in a straight blonde wig as 'Celebrity Illusionist - Simone Phoenix', the 'New Star Attraction for Summer 2018'. On closer inspection, Julia realised she was impersonating Cher in the picture, the resemblance so uncanny that she was surprised she had not immediately spotted it.

"Well, this is certainly different," Julia said with a smile as she rang the doorbell on the locked interior door.

The door flung open almost immediately to reveal a tall man with slicked back brown hair and half a face of elaborate makeup. His features had been chiselled out with dark powder, and his eyes looked three times the size of a regular humans thanks to smoky black shadow and thick, lustrous lashes. He had outlined the exaggerated shape for his lips but had yet to fill them in. To contrast with the beautiful makeup, he was wearing a plain white T-shirt and faded jeans.

"You'll have to excuse my half-done face, dear," the man exclaimed as he took in Julia's pink and blue floral summer dress. "Oh, I say! You've come in our signature colours, and you look beautiful. I count four frightened faces, so I'm going to go out on a limb and guess that you dears are the competition winners. Well, don't just stand out there all day. Come in! I don't like leaving the door open. It lets the fun leak out."

The tall man took Julia's bag from her and held open the door as they walked into the hallway, which had been decorated in bright pink and blue leopard print pattern wallpaper. Framed pictures of cabaret stage performances lined the walls to the reception desk at the end of the hall.

"From your expressions, I'm going to assume you've never heard of Sparkles by the Sea," the man announced as he walked around the desk, which also happened to be a large tank housing dozens of colourful fish. "My name is Russell Braithwaite, also known as Lulu Suede when I'm in full drag, and I am the proud owner of this establishment. I'll hold for applause." Russell held out his hands, but none of them clapped. "Tough crowd. I'm joking, dears. The looks on your faces!" Russell chuckled to himself as he typed something into a laptop on the desk. "I've been the owner of Sparkles for ten years now, for my sins. I bought the place from the legendary Cream Cake Devour shortly before her death, may she rest in peace. Sparkles has been providing clean, family friendly drag fun to Blackpool for over thirty years. If you want the raunchy stuff, you'll have to go further into the dark streets for that. We're all about entertaining your kids and your granny at the same time here, and if you leave your political correctness at the door, we do just that. We're not only a popular bed and breakfast with impeccable standards, but we also provide world class all day entertainment in our cabaret bar. Honey, our youngest queen, is currently in there amusing with drag bingo."

"Drag bingo?" Barker asked. "What's that?"

"Well, it's normal bingo, but the announcer is in drag," Russell explained flatly. "Don't worry, dear, you'll catch up eventually. You've arrived just in time for my ice cream brunch. And before you ask, it's where you all sit down and eat delicious ice cream while I tell jokes. That's what Lulu Suede does. I'm a comedian. Honey is our artsy young queen who thinks she's good enough for a single name, but that never stopped Madonna or Adele, did it?"

"And Drake," Jessie added.

"Who, dear?" Russell asked as he continued to type before his eyes drifted to something behind them. "*Ah*! This is Feather Duster, our old, old, old, old, old veteran queen."

They all turned to look at a short, plump drag queen in a sequin dress and a short grey curly wig as she walked through the front door.

"You missed off an extra old," Feather Duster said with a wave of her hand as she slipped through a door that led to the bar.

"Our Feather Duster has been here since the day Sparkles opened in 1988, and some say she was even hanging around outside before we opened. Nobody knows exactly how old Feather Duster is, but we assume she was there for the invention of the wheel. She won't let me cut her in half to count the rings, so it remains a mystery." Russell finished typing and looked up. "We also have Simone Phoenix, our newest Sparkles recruit. She's a fabulous celebrity impersonator who headlines our nightly cabaret show. I highly recommend you see her in action tonight. We also have Tuna Turner. We started in drag together at the same dingy backstreet bar almost twenty years ago. It's been turned into a coffee shop now, but it's probably for the best. She's our resident fishy queen."

"Fishy queen?" Julia asked.

"Fishy queens are drag queens who look like real women," Russell explained. "So, the opposite of what I do. I'm a clown. I like to make people laugh and look silly doing it. It takes Tuna two hours to paint her face, and I can do mine in half an hour in a pinch. I keep her around to admire her beauty, and we go way back. If you see an incredibly beautiful woman with an attitude problem, it's probably Tuna. Now, you know who we are, but I have no idea who you beautiful people are. I spoke to a lady called Dot on the phone, but none of you looks like a 'Dot' to me."

"I'm Julia, and this is my fiancé, Barker," Julia said, stepping to the side to reveal Jessie and Alfie. "This is our soon-to-be adopted daughter, Jessie, and her older brother, Alfie. Alfie took Dot's place. She's come down with a cold so she couldn't make it."

"How modern!" Russell exclaimed before hitting one final key on the laptop. "You'll fit right into our colourful family. All jokes aside, if you need anything at all, please don't be afraid to ask. For a bunch of old queens, we pride ourselves on our professionalism and hospitality. Breakfast is served at eight sharp in the restaurant to my right, and there's always something happening in the bar to my left, so don't be afraid to venture inside. We don't bite, much. Julia and Barker, I'm putting you in the Liza Minnelli suite, and Jessie and Alfie, you are in the Madonna twin room next door."

Russell handed over two sets of keys, both of which had their respective celebrity themes printed on the plastic room number keyring.

"Have fun, join in, and don't take it too seriously!" Russell announced, clapping his hands together. "There's a lift through the restaurant. You're up on the top floor. You can't miss your rooms."

Julia picked up her bag as the door to the bar opened. A young drag queen in a David Bowie-style orange mullet wig walked out in a sheer gold mesh shirt with flared black trousers.

"I'm going to *kill* her, Lulu!" the queen announced as she leaned against the wall. "Simone's just told me she's bumping my routine down to the second slot tonight. She's trying to push me out! She knows it doesn't work there in the show. I always go on before she does!"

"*Guests*, Honey," Russell said, nodding to the quartet. "Excuse her. She's eighteen and hasn't realised the world doesn't revolve around her yet." Russell turned to Honey, a stern expression underneath his makeup-caked face. "Honey, go and take a smoke break, and come back with your attitude in check. You're a boy in a wig. It doesn't all have to be this serious."

Honey rolled her eyes and stomped down the corridor towards the entrance. Russell smiled apologies to his guests.

"They say never work with children and animals, but I say, never work with drag queens," he said. "It ages you. I'm only forty-two, but I look eighty-seven under this cake face. If you can find your rooms on your own, I'll have to excuse myself. The ice cream brunch starts in ten minutes, and as usual, I'm nowhere near ready."

With that, Russell headed through a door behind the desk, leaving them to walk through a 1950s American diner themed restaurant to the lift as instructed.

"I don't think we know what we've let ourselves in for," Barker said with an awkward laugh as he looked around the diner.

"I think this is going to be fun," Julia replied. "Dot doesn't know what she's missing."

"Or maybe she does," Jessie said quietly, her eyes darting from side to side as she looked around the empty diner. "Let's not forget Evelyn's prophecy."

But Julia had forgotten all about Evelyn's prophecy. She looked around the restaurant as the lift descended from a higher level, wondering what 'darkness' Evelyn had sensed in a place that was clearly intent on bringing happiness. Julia had never put much stock into vague prophecies, but Evelyn had fully believed her words when handing over the envelope. The reminder from Jessie had planted a small seed of something in the back of Julia's mind that was making her look at the joyfully decorated B&B with slightly different eyes. She shook her head, determined not to let a vague warning of 'darkness' ruin their break.

"We're going to have fun," Julia repeated firmly as the lift doors slid open. "You'll see."

CHAPTER 3

A fter leaving their bags in the celebrity-themed bedrooms, they spent the rest of the afternoon exploring Blackpool. They started by eating the largest portions of fish and chips any of them had ever seen at a chippy on the corner before taking a stroll along Central Pier. After spending a small fortune in the amusement arcade on the pier, they visited the large *Sea Life* aquarium, then grabbed ice cream from a van on the side of the road before heading back to their rooms to get ready for the evening show. Evelyn's warning of 'darkness' was already a distant memory.

By the time Julia was back in the Liza Minnelli suite, she felt well and truly relaxed. Her apprehension about leaving Peridale had vanished.

Staring at the giant mural of Liza in her spotlight against a red backdrop in her Cabaret outfit, Julia was tempted to call Katie to see how her first day had gone. She got as far as hovering over her name on her phone, but she decided to leave it for the time being. Even though she still had her doubts, she was sure someone in the village would have called if something disastrous had happened. She made a mental note to call on Sunday when Katie had worked through two full days.

After Barker walked out of the en-suite bathroom with a large pink towel hugging his hips, Julia jumped into the shower and washed the day away. The hours of driving and salty sea air had played havoc with her chocolaty curls, making her glad that the shower was hot and powerful. When she was squeaky clean, she pulled on one of the complimentary fuzzy pink dressing gowns.

Barker was writing at the table next to the window, still only wearing a towel around his waist. With the curtains open, they had a perfect view of the sea.

"It looks like you could fall right off the edge," Julia said as she ran a small towel through her dripping hair. "I always wondered what it would be like to live by the seaside."

A seagull dove past the window, squawking as it went. Barker sighed and dropped his pen before pinching between his eyes. He pushed the small book away with a huff.

"It's like trying to draw blood from a stone," he said, rubbing his neck as though he had just done a workout. "Do you think it's too late to beg for my job back at the station?"

Julia tilted her head to read what he had written. 'Drag queens by the sea. Fish and chips. Aquarium'. His publisher had recommended that he write his thoughts and experiences in a journal to help prompt his writing.

"Still having a block?" she asked, gazing in the direction of Central Pier as the Ferris wheel slowly turned.

"I'm starting to think the first book was a fluke," he said, staring darkly at the journal. "I can't form a simple sentence about my day."

Julia sat at the dressing table and watched Barker through the mirror as he rubbed the creases in his forehead. Ever since the release of his first crime novel a month ago, he had been struggling with the process of the follow-up. With the whole country enjoying Barker's first effort, he seemed to be suffering from the pressure of making lightning strike twice. Now that the press hype had died down, Barker had time to sit and write again away from the cameras, but he had yet to produce anything without deleting it immediately after.

"When I bake a great cake that everyone loves, I always worry when I have to make another," Julia said with a soft smile when his eyes met hers in the mirror. "I find letting go of that expectation is the only way to get through it. Don't compare, just create. If you enjoy what you're producing, other people will too."

Barker nodded his understanding and picked up the pen again. He continued writing for a second before sighing and snapping his journal shut.

"I'll come back to it tomorrow," he said before jumping up. "Maybe tonight's show will get my creative cogs turning again."

"You should write your next book about killer drag queens," Julia joked as she searched the drawers to find a hairdryer. "They could be killed by arsenic in the eyeshadow, or an exploding wig."

"I don't think the publishers would *quite* go for that." Barker opened the wardrobe and pulled out a pale blue shirt. "Is this too much?"

"I don't think it's enough." Julia chuckled. "You could always borrow one of my dresses. You'll fit right in. They might even ask you to get up and do a little number."

"I'll leave that to the professionals." Barker put the shirt back and pulled out one of his usual plain white ones. "I'll play it safe tonight. I have all week to experiment with colour."

Julia reached the bottom drawer where there was a notice letting her know to ask reception for a hairdryer. Julia looked around for a phone to call down, but there did not seem to be one. Leaving Barker to pick between his almost identical white shirts, she pushed her feet into the matching pink slippers before making her way down the hallway to the lift at the end. When the elevator reached the ground floor, the doors opened onto the full restaurant. Julia looked down at her dressing gown and pulled it tighter together. She nearly went back up to her room to put some clothes on, but people were already giving her strange looks. With an awkward smile, she hurried across the diner, keeping her hands firmly on the front of the gown to stop it fluttering open.

The reception desk was unmanned, but there was a glittery pink doorbell on the wall. She was about to press it when the door behind the fish tank counter opened slightly. She stepped to the side and saw Russell holding the door open with his back to Julia. In front of him stood a tall drag queen unmistakably dressed as Dolly Parton in a signature white jumpsuit and giant blonde wig.

"Just go and get ready for your show," Russell demanded, the charm and happiness from earlier absent in his voice. "I'm not going through this again, Simone."

Simone Phoenix, the celebrity illusionist, walked to the open door, but she stopped directly in front of

Russell's face. Russell was tall, but Simone towered over Russell in her heels.

"You've got a bad memory, Russell," the drag queen hissed in his face. "Let's not forget how empty this place was before I came here. You were on the edge. Simone Phoenix *is* the star. I saved this place. People come to see me."

"You're not irreplaceable. Nobody is."

"If I go, the people *will* follow me to wherever I work next. I gave you a good deal because of our history, but the trial period is over. Increase my salary, or I walk."

Simone marched out of the small office and past Julia without so much as a glance in her direction. Simone picked up a guitar that was leaning against the wall and walked into the bar. Julia hovered for a moment, unsure of what to do. The office door closed again, so she rang the doorbell. Russell appeared seconds later with a wide grin, showing no signs of the conflict that she had just witnessed. Julia was impressed by how good an actor he was.

"That's certainly a *look*," Russell said as he took in the dressing gown. "Although I have to say, I preferred the dress you were wearing this afternoon.

Hairdryer?"

"Yes, please," Julia said, feeling her cheeks blush as she pulled the gown together even tighter. "I think I forgot I wasn't at home for a moment."

"That's what I like to hear." Russell opened the office door and nodded for Julia to follow him inside. "C'mon. Let's get you away from prying eyes. People will start questioning what kind of establishment I'm running."

Julia hurried into the office, grateful for Russell's humour. Out of drag and with a clean face, Julia could see how classically handsome he was. Despite his earlier remark about looking double his age, he was faring better than some forty-two-year-olds Julia had met.

"Welcome to my drag den," Russell said before walking over to a tall cupboard labelled 'hairdryers'. "People kept stealing them because they were pretty and pink."

Julia accepted the glowing hairdryer as she looked around the room. Even though it functioned as some sort of office, it was evidently much more than that. One of the walls was covered entirely in shelves packed with wigs on plastic heads, every style and shade of the rainbow represented. The opposite wall had two long rails, one on top of the other, both crammed floor to ceiling with sparkly gowns and flamboyant costumes. Bright makeup cluttered the counter on the far wall, which had a vanity mirror with similar lights to those that outlined the door outside. In the soft glow, Julia's skin looked more perfect than she had ever seen it. Russell appeared behind her and pulled up her brows slightly.

"I knew it," he said with a confident nod. "You'd suit a sharp wing. You have the bones for it, dear. Not everyone does. You are really beautiful, Julia. I can tell you have a face that can take makeup."

"I never really wear it," Julia admitted as she looked at herself in the mirror. "A little mascara and maybe a lip tint if I'm in the mood."

"But you'd look utterly gorgeous!" Russell announced, pushing her into a chair in front of the mirror. "You *must* let me paint you, dear. *Nay*! I insist! It's an hour until show time, which gives me half an hour to play."

"Oh, that's not necessary," Julia said with a shake of her head. "I really appreciate the offer, but -"

Julia attempted to stand up, but Russell pushed

her back into the chair and spun her away from the mirror. He had a playful smirk that made her feel like he was plotting a devious plan.

"It wasn't a question, dear," Russell replied as he clipped Julia's wet hair away from her face. "It's just dirt with pigments. If you don't like it, you can wash it off. I might paint myself like a clown, but I do know my way around a woman's face. I gave makeovers at a department store for years on the side before buying this place."

Russell applied light moisturiser before squirting pale foundation onto a glass palette. He bounced the product around her face with a pink sponge before setting it with dusty white powder. Without the aid of the mirror, she could only imagine what he was doing to her face, and even though he had assured her he knew what he was doing, she could see the half-finished exaggerated face that had greeted her on arrival that afternoon.

Like an artist working on a painting, Russell danced brushes across her face, pausing to assess his work. He worked at whirlwind speed, switching between products, his smile widening as he grew closer and closer to completing his masterpiece. After pulling up her brows to apply eyeshadow, he skilfully gave her a coat of mascara before gluing on false lashes.

"Do they always feel this heavy?" Julia asked as she blinked, suddenly more aware of her eyes than she ever had been.

"You should try wearing mine," he replied as he outlined her lips with lipstick. "I stack four pairs. They could kick up a wind stiff enough to rid Blackpool beach of its sand. Pout for me, dear."

Julia did as she was told. Russell nodded his satisfaction and stepped back with a pleased grin. He squirted something from a bottle all over her face before popping open a hand fan with a flourish and wafting her skin. When he was satisfied, he spun her around in the chair.

"You don't have to close your eyes," he said as he spread something through her still damp hair. "Just have a look and be honest."

Julia opened her eyes, uncertain of what she was going to see. She stared ahead at the mirror, her eyes instantly darting up to Russell, his pleased grin growing. Instead of seeing a clown, she saw the face of a striking 1940s star.

"There are wipes on the side if you want to do your own thing," Russell said as he plugged in the hairdryer. "I just like to play."

Julia looked at the wipes, but she had no intention of wiping it off; she never wanted to take it off. As Russell blow-dried her hair, she edged closer to the mirror. Her skin looked fresh but had angles she had never seen before. Her cheeks glowed in an ethereal way, as did her sparkly eyelids. Her brows had somehow taken on a near-perfect shape, as had her lips. Even though she could feel the lashes, they looked natural in the mirror.

"I don't know what to say," Julia said, turning her head from side to side. "I've never seen myself like this before. I look –"

"Beautiful," Russell called over the sound of the hairdryer. "That's the word you're looking for, dear. I said to myself, 'Russell, paint her like she's a young Hedy Lamarr'."

"Hedy Lamarr?"

"A 1940s Austrian film star," Russell said. "She was incredibly beautiful. She married six times, but she died alone and a recluse, a telephone her only means of communication with the outside world.

Probably for the best because she turned to plastic surgery to preserve her looks and ended up looking like a melted Barbie doll, but isn't that always the way? Quite a fabulous woman."

"She sounds like a character."

"She was," Russell replied with a distant smile. "Sometimes I feel like I'm destined to become her, but I think most drag queens do. It's our curse to be filled with pointless pop culture knowledge, and yet we rarely have people to share it with when we're not entertaining on the stage. Not many people can look past the art form to see the person underneath."

Julia was troubled to hear that someone so focussed on entertaining other people could feel so alone, especially in a full B&B. She was drawn to Russell in a way she had not expected to be from their first meeting. She liked him, and she could sense his goodness as well as his sadness.

The minutes passed by as he finished blow-drying her hair into perfect waves. He applied some hairspray and something to make it shiny before declaring that he was finished. As Julia stared at herself in the mirror, she could barely believe she was looking at her own reflection.

"I look like my mother," Julia said, her voice barely above a whisper. "People always said I looked like her, but I never really saw it until now."

"Your mother must also have been beautiful."

"You're a wizard!" Julia was unable to look away from herself. "I can't believe you did all of this in half an hour."

"Fifty minutes, actually," he said after checking his watch. "Which leaves me ten to get ready."

"Oh," Julia said as she got out of his seat. "I'm sorry, I didn't –"

"Don't *apologise!* You were my beauty hostage, and it was worth every second. I'll just do my quick face. Dark eyes and I'll grab a wig with a fringe. I'm the host, so people's eyes will be turned to the stage." Russell sat down and started to run a stick foundation across his face. "Now that I've chewed your ear off, you'll want to get back to your fiancé. He'll be thinking I kidnapped you."

Julia nodded and turned to walk away, but she remembered what Russell had said about rarely having anyone to talk to outside of his drag world.

"I'd quite like to see how you do your face," Julia said, trying to sound as casual as possible. "Maybe I can pick up a few tips?"

"You *don't* want to copy *any* of my tips," Russell pulled up a stack of crates next to his chair, draped a pink glittery piece of fabric across it, and patted for Julia to sit. "Do you like piña coladas?"

CHAPTER 4

Two piña coladas, two mystery pink shots, and half an hour later, Julia walked as smoothly as she could along the corridor to her room. Russell transformed into Lulu Suede before they had finished their first cocktail, but he pushed show time back and persuaded Honey to play another round of drag bingo to ease the crowd.

Realising she had been gone for well over an hour,

Julia pried open the door, not wanting to startle Barker. To her surprise, he was still by the window in his towel, pen scribbling in his journal.

"Sorry I took so long," Julia said, trying to hide that she was a little tipsy. "Russell offered to do my makeup and hair."

"*Huh?*" Barker mumbled, his pen still gliding across the paper. "Sorry. I had an idea. I had to write it down before it vanished." Barker glanced up at Julia, but he quickly returned to his work. "You look nice."

Julia pulled out a daring red dress she had never worn. It had been a Christmas present from her sister, who had a habit of buying her glamorous clothes she never had a use for. She had only packed it on a whim. After grabbing underwear from her case, she ripped the tags off the dress and disappeared into the bathroom with instructions for Barker to get ready. Five minutes later, she emerged feeling like a new woman.

"Blooming heck, Julia!" Jessie cried when Julia knocked on her bedroom door. "You *are* Julia, aren't you? You look like you were abducted by aliens."

"I think she's trying to say you look gorgeous,"

Alfie offered from behind his sister. "New dress?"

"It's just a little something," Julia said, brushing down the front, unsure of how she felt about how tight it was. "Should I change?"

"*No!*" Jessie and Alfie replied in unison.

Barker joined them after finally dressing. He locked the door and turned to Julia, taking in her transformation for the first time without the distraction of writing. He opened and closed his mouth, a small throaty sound escaping. Alfie slapped him on the shoulder as he walked past, and Jessie shook her head.

"Has anyone ever told you that you look just like Hedy Lamarr?" Barker asked, the words sounding foreign as they left his mouth. "Before the scary plastic surgery."

"That's surprisingly not the first time I've heard that today," Julia said, arching a brow as she looked sceptically at Barker. "How do you know who Hedy Lamarr is?"

"My mum was obsessed with the black and white movies," Barker said, his eyes dancing up and down the red dress. "Did you know Hedy invented Bluetooth and Wi-Fi technology in the 1940s during the Second World War?"

"I didn't," Julia said, impressed by the fact. "You're full of surprises, Barker Brown."

Holding her head high, Julia let Barker lead her down the hallway to the lift where Alfie and Jessie were waiting. After descending to the ground floor, they walked through the full restaurant. This time, she garnered slightly different looks than the ones she had got when walking through in a pink dressing gown with wet hair. Julia knew it was an illusion that would vanish when she showered later, but for now, she felt worlds apart from that woman who had been in search of a hairdryer. As she walked towards the cabaret bar with all eyes on her, she understood the appeal of transforming oneself into a new person entirely.

The bar was themed similarly to their bedroom. A grand stage with a single spotlight and red velvet backdrop commanded attention. Honey was on a stool in the spotlight pulling bingo balls from a basket and announcing them unenthusiastically. Small tables with candle lamps filled the space all the way to the bar at the back of the room. The place was packed out, with all tables full apart from one table at the front with a 'RESERVED' sign. Julia was about to walk over to the back when Russell, now dressed as Lulu Suede, caught her eye from the DJ booth and nodded at the one remaining table.

Feeling like she had made a friend in Russell and Lulu, Julia appreciatively took the table. As though someone up on high had read her mind, a tray with four sparkler-topped piña coladas appeared. When Jessie reached out for one, Julia arched one of her defined brows.

"I'm on *holiday!*" Jessie cried, taking a sip of the frothy cocktail before anyone could snatch it off her. "And I'm eighteen on Friday! One week until I'm legal to drink. You're not going to make me drink pop for the sake of a week, are you?"

"You couldn't get served at a bar," Alfie reminded her. "That week makes the difference."

"And I'm an ex-detective inspector," Barker said, winking at Julia before frowning at Jessie. "Do you think I can sit by and let this happen?"

Jessie's mouth opened as though she was about to launch into a squabble, but they burst out laughing, causing her cheeks to darken.

"I don't even want it now anyway," she muttered,

folding her arms. "Tastes like a rubbish pineapple milkshake."

Despite Jessie's protests, she finished the drink along with the rest of them. Julia trusted her, and she was under no illusion that it was Jessie's first alcoholic drink. She knew Jessie was sensible, and they were on holiday after all. After ordering their second round of drinks from a handsome waiter in a bowtie, the lights dimmed. Julia looked to Lulu in her booth next to the stage as she picked up a microphone.

"Ladies and gentlemen, welcome to Sparkles by the Sea's world-famous nightly cabaret show!" Lulu announced, her voice travelling through the speakers dotted about the club. "My name is Lulu Suede. Why 'Suede' I hear you ask? Because suede is softer than leather, and I'm as soft as they come, just don't get too close or you'll see the stubble poking through the spackled-on makeup on my chin. Do you know what hot new tool drag queens are using to apply their makeup? A trowel." Lulu paused for a smattering of laughter. "I'd recommend it, ladies. It gets the job done in seconds, and by the looks of it, some of you need a little extra help tonight." Lulu paused again, the laughter growing. "I won't apologise for being late. I was having a cosmetic procedure done out back. I asked the surgeon to turn back the hands of time, but instead, he gave me a face that could stop the clocks." Lulu pressed something on the laptop under the booth, and a *ba dum tss!* drum sting crackled through the speakers. "Thank you, thank you! That's about the standard of jokes you're going to get tonight, so I'd suggest grabbing the nearest waiter and asking for a strong drink. I hope you're all strapped in and ready for an amazing night of cabaret. Our first act is so old, they've cancelled her blood type, her last cake had more candles than actual cake, and when she was at school, they didn't have history lessons because nothing had actually happened yet. She says she's still got it, but it's a question of if anyone actually wants to see it, and I know I don't. Ladies and gentlemen, please give a warm welcome and a loud round of applause, especially because I've turned off her hearing aids, for Blackpool's very own prehistoric fossilised specimen, *Feather Duster!*"

Applause and laughter erupted around the room as Feather Duster shuffled into the spotlight where Honey's bingo stool was waiting for her. She flashed Lulu a grin, letting everyone know the teasing was in good fun. Under the makeup and costume, it was hard to determine the drag queen's true age, but Julia would have guessed whoever was under the costume was past retiring age. A piano track started, and Feather performed a beautiful rendition of *Somewhere Over the Rainbow.*

As Julia watched Feather sing, she was transported to another era. Feather's weathered and mature voice provided a grit that reminded Julia of Judy Garland's later years. When Feather started *When You Wish Upon a Star,* the whole audience, including those at Julia's table, was right behind her. Jessie and Alfie both shared the same captivated expression as Feather sang, as did Barker. *Moon River* came next, followed by *Let's Call The Whole Thing Off,* and finally, *Diamonds Are A Girl's Best Friend,* for which Feather stood up and shimmied around the stage. When it came time for her final bow, the vigorous applause that consumed the room was almost deafening. Feather shuffled off the stage as though it was nothing more than a day at the office, making Julia wonder if the person under the makeup even knew what kind of talent they had.

As the applause eased and Lulu lifted the mic up

to her mouth, there was a brief moment of silence. In the quiet, Julia heard shrill, raised voices coming from behind the stage area. She glanced at Lulu who seemed to have heard it too, but being the professional that she was, she pressed a button, and soft background music drowned it out.

"Wasn't that beautiful?" Lulu called, her eyes looking beyond the curtain thanks to her vantage point in the raised booth. "I'm afraid that was Feather Duster's *final* performance. The grim reaper is waiting backstage to drag her off to the underworld, and it's long overdue if you ask me. I was the one who called him. I did call The Pope first to perform an exorcism, but he said this case was beyond even his powers. The demon within our poor old Feather Duster has too strong a hold on her, but at least it's operating her corpse for your entertainment. Of course, I'm joking, ladies and gentlemen. Feather Duster will, of course, be back tomorrow night and *every* night here at Sparkles by the Sea. She's the original Sparkle Girl. She'll out-live us all and still be here with Cher and the cockroaches after the inevitable and impending nuclear war."

Lulu paused for another drum sting, not that it

was necessary. The crowd cackled along with her jokes, no doubt thanks to the flowing alcohol. Julia looked down at her empty glass, wondering how many piña coladas she had so far enjoyed.

"And now we go from one end of the age spectrum to the other," Lulu announced after a pause to sip her drink. "If Feather Duster was born just after The Big Bang, I'd say our next performer was born…" Lulu checked her watch. "…about five minutes ago. She's barely out of nappies, and she's only *just* said her first word, but that's not stopping her throwing on a wig to get out here to perform for you tonight. If she looks a little dazed and confused it's because her brain hasn't fully developed yet. You've heard the stereotypes about today's kids being entitled, lazy, and stupid, and our next performer is here to prove they're *all* absolutely true. Put your hands together for Honey!"

Honey strutted onto the stage in a pair of impossibly tall heels, dragging a metal chair behind her. She glared at Lulu, not seeming to have the same sense of humour as Feather. She was wearing the same orange mullet as before, but she had painted her entire face pink with white dots everywhere. It was a striking and beautiful look, even if the message was lost on Julia. She barely resembled a woman like the other queens, her image appearing to bend and blur the lines between genders.

Instead of singing live, Honey displayed her acrobatic skills by balancing on the chair in various positions while music pounded through the bar. Julia caught Jessie and Alfie giving each other sceptical looks as they watched Honey's performance. When she was finished, she stormed off stage without taking a bow.

"As I said, ladies and gents," Lulu said, obvious frustration in her voice. "Proving all those stereotypes to be correct. You can find Honey's next performance in the back alley behind the job centre next week. Remind me to loosen the screws on that chair for tomorrow night's performance. That might make for a more *interesting* piece. We're going to have a short, unscheduled interval, but we'll be back with more cabaret after the break."

Lulu turned the music up loud and stormed across the stage, vanishing behind the curtain. Julia craned her neck to see what was happening, but Lulu had turned off the spotlight and plunged the stage into darkness.

"I'm having more fun than I expected," Barker called over the music. "Who knew a drag show could be fun?"

"They're a riot," Alfie said, slurping up the last of his cocktail. "I've seen them all over the world. It's always the best night out. Nobody will make you laugh like a British drag queen though. That Lulu knows her way around a microphone."

"It's like dad jokes, but they're funny," Jessie said, her eyes a little woozy as she peered into her empty glass. "Where did my drink go?"

"You drank it," Julia said, pulling it away from her. "You've had enough for tonight. Pop next!"

Jessie huffed and crossed her arms before pulling out her phone. The brightness of the screen almost made her fall out of her chair.

"We're on holiday," Barker reminded Julia. "But you're probably right about the pop. Those cocktails are deceptive."

Julia heard something crash backstage and jolted her attention back to the curtain. It fluttered enough to show Honey and Simone face to face, as though they were about to start fighting. A minute later, Lulu reappeared, looking a little dishevelled and red-faced. She announced that Tuna Turner would be up next without the comedic introduction she had given the first two performers.

Tuna walked onto the stage, and for a moment, Julia thought a real woman had jumped up to have a go. Her beauty was breath-taking, her rich dark skin and striking features reminding Julia of Naomi Campbell. Tuna performed an energetic dance routine to a Britney Spears mix of songs before Lulu passed her a microphone. She announced that she needed a volunteer, her eyes landing straight on Barker. Even though he protested, Jessie and Alfie pushed him up, and Tuna dragged him onto the stage and sat him in a chair. Julia found herself cheering, even though Barker looked like a deer in the headlights.

Throughout a lip-synced performance of Shania Twain's *Man! I feel Like A Woman*, Tuna quickly dressed Barker in drag. By the end of the song, he was wearing poorly applied lipstick, a wonky wig, a loose dress over his shirt and jeans, all complete with an embarrassed and humiliated expression.

"Smile for the camera!" Jessie cried, pointing her

phone in his face when he wandered back to their table. "I can't wait to post this!"

Before Barker could say anything, Lulu picked up the microphone, laughing at Barker, just as she had been throughout the number.

"Wasn't he *brilliant*, folks?" Lulu announced before clapping in Barker's direction. "Once again proving that anyone *can* do drag, but not everyone *should*. If you go with Honey, dear, she'll get you cleaned up and give you a drink on the house for being a good sport."

Honey appeared and led Barker out of the bar by his hand. He followed like a lost puppy, glancing back at Julia as though asking for help. She gave him two thumbs up, her spirits too high to take his wounded look seriously.

"Isn't this *great*?" Julia called over the music to Jessie and Alfie. "I'm having the best time!"

"So am I after *that*," Jessie said, chuckling at her phone. "And, it's uploaded! I'm never letting Barker live that down."

"Poor fella," Alfie tittered with a shake of his head. "He's definitely going to need that free drink."

Lulu announced that the star attraction for the

summer, Simone Phoenix, would be up very soon. The mere mention of her name caused the loudest applause yet, with some people whooping and whistling. Julia looked back at the bar, which was twice as busy as it had been for Feather Duster's opening act. As Julia looked out for Barker's return, the lights cut off, making Julia wonder if there had been a technical glitch. Seconds later, lasers and smoke suddenly filled the stage, and Simone, dressed as Dolly Parton, strutted into the spotlight. The noise coming from the bar behind Julia was crushingly loud, making her wonder what was so unique about the celebrity illusionist. She remembered what she had overheard Simone say to Russell earlier, and her new-found friendship with Russell made her dislike Simone. As she started her Dolly lip-syncing routine accompanied with fake guitar playing, Julia looked to the DJ booth, but Lulu had vanished; she had been there throughout all the other performances.

The first song, *Islands in the Stream*, drifted by without Julia paying much attention. Simone ran off stage while the music still played, and ran back on less than thirty seconds later, magically transformed from Dolly into Cher. After a spot-on performance of

Believe, Julia found her interest levels rising. She assumed the alcohol was helping blur the lines, but the illusion had sucked her in. Another quick costume change turned her into Madonna during her cone bra era for a performance of *Express Yourself* with eerily accurate dance moves. Another quick change transformed her into Freddie Mercury from the *I Want to Break Free* music video, complete with a comical vacuum cleaner and moustache. After running off the stage again, Simone returned after the longest break dressed as an 80s Cyndi Lauper, this time with a live microphone.

"I wonder where Barker is," Julia whispered to Jessie and Alfie as Simone sipped a drink before putting it on the edge of the stage. "He's been gone for ages."

"He's probably being held hostage by the drag queens," Jessie said, her thumbs tapping away on her phone. "Two hundred views already! Everyone is commenting."

"Do you want me to go and look for him?" Alfie offered.

"No," Julia replied quickly. "He's probably just gone back to the room."

She turned back to the stage as Simone held the microphone up to her mouth. The backing track had ended with the last song, and something told Julia it was supposed to be the end of her set.

"Thank you, everyone," Simone cooed into the microphone, clearly out of breath from all the running around. "I'd be nothing without my fans."

The applause started up again. It seemed Simone's claim about her name filling the bar had been correct. Julia looked around for Lulu, but she was nowhere to be seen, nor were any of the other performers.

"For the first time in my career, I'm going to be singing live for you," Simone announced with a nervous grin. "It's something I've always wanted to do, and tonight is the night I realise that dream. If you know the words, help me out and sing along."

Without a backing track, Simone started singing *True Colours* with the assistance of the audience. Even though Julia's mind was foggy from the rum in the cocktails, her ears were functioning. She winced as Simone struggled to hit any notes in the song. She looked around, but no one seemed to notice as they sung along at the top of their lungs, likely too drunk to care either way.

"Who killed the cat?" Jessie called out. "Bring back the old woman! She could *sing*!"

Simone grew louder and louder, and by the final chorus, she was practically shouting down the microphone. At that moment, Barker walked back in, the dress, wig, and lipstick gone.

"It stained my face," he explained as he sat down. "I had to go up to the room to scrub it off."

He pulled his chair back in, thankfully not too scarred from his public performance. He sipped his drink, wincing as he looked at the stage as Simone repeated the final chorus.

"She's *murdering* this!" Barker cried, his face scrunched up. "Some people just can't –"

Before Barker could finish his sentence, there was a metallic groan from somewhere above the stage. It was loud enough to silence Simone, but not to stop the rest of the bar from singing aloud. As the crowd sang '*I see your true colours, and that's why I love you*' at the top of their lungs, Julia watched in horror as the triangular lighting rig above Simone's head swung down. As though in slow motion, Julia watched Simone stare at the rig as it flew towards her.

Before she had a chance to move, it hit the performer with the force of a bus. She flew backwards and landed with a crash in the smoke. A confused silence fell over the bar before the ceiling lights were turned on, blinding Julia. When her eyes adjusted, she stared at the metallic scaffolding hanging down, its sizzling and crackling lights dangling in the silence.

Julia jumped out of her seat, realising what had happened. With her hand over her mouth, she stepped forward as the smoke cleared. First, she saw Cyndi Lauper's orange spiky wig hanging off the edge of the stage, and then she saw the wide, vacant eyes of Simone Phoenix staring back at her, the microphone still clutched in her hand. Julia was about to exclaim that the drag queen was dead, but her heart stopped when Simone blinked, her eyes locked with Julia's.

"Call an ambulance!" Julia cried into the crowd. "*Now!*"

ICE CREAM AND INCIDENTS

CHAPTER 5

The mood in the diner was sombre the following morning. Julia finished her entire full English breakfast without even realising she was eating. Her mind was too absorbed by what had happened to focus on food. Simone, who went by Simon Blair out of drag, was in hospital and had somehow survived the blow from the collapsed rig. The look on Russell's face when he delivered a vague update to the packed restaurant at the start of breakfast told Julia that Simon's condition was as yet far from stable.

Before the guests fled the diner, Russell sent Honey around with a box to collect donations to 'buy Simon the biggest bunch of flowers money can buy for when he wakes up'. When Honey reached their table, Julia pulled out a crisp ten-pound note, as did Barker. Out of drag, Honey was a strikingly beautiful boy with unusual grey eyes and bright red short curly hair. He was wearing a slightly cropped top to show off his slender, toned midriff, along with tight jeans with more holes than denim.

"Do you have a real name?" Jessie asked as she tossed a couple of coins into the box. "For when you're in boy mode, I mean."

"Honey," he replied as he rattled the box at Alfie, prompting him to dig for his wallet in his jeans. "My mum's a weirdo."

Alfie dropped a five-pound note into the box before Honey moved onto the next table. Julia observed him as he shook the donations box, the distance in his strangely pale eyes showing that his mind was somewhere else. She wondered if he was thinking about how he had announced that he was going to 'kill Simone' for moving his chair performance down in the billing just hours before the rig fell.

"I feel bad for saying Simone was murdering that song last night," Barker muttered as he pushed leftover beans around his plate. "I could have chosen better words."

"She *was* awful," Jessie said with a roll of her eyes. "Let's not pretend the queen could sing because she couldn't." Jessie paused and looked across the table at Julia, her dark eyes pinning her into the chair. "What do y*ou* think, Julia?"

"About Simone's singing?"

"About this whole thing," Jessie said, lowering her voice as she leaned in. "Don't you think it's all a little – *weird?*"

Julia had been able to think of nothing else. 'Tragic accident' and 'wrong place, wrong time' had been batted around more times than a ball at a tennis match all morning. She knew it was possible, and it sounded like the most plausible explanation for what had happened, but Jessie was right, there was something weird about how it had happened.

"It felt theatrical," Barker mused, almost to himself as he rattled his knife between his fingers. "Like a grand finale to the show."

"That's *exactly* what was weird about it," Jessie said, snapping her fingers together. "It felt too perfect. If it was just an accident, it could have fallen at any point during the show."

"Coincidence?" Alfie offered.

"No such thing," Jessie said, dismissing him with a wave of her hand. "Julia probably has it all figured out already, don't you? Or do we need to split up and start questioning people?"

Julia admired Jessie's spirit. Despite being curious as to what had happened, she was not sure there was much to look into. A 'weird' feeling was hardly the basis for an investigation, and it was probably the most expected reaction after witnessing something so strange. Simon was alive and in hospital, and the obvious answer seemed to fit. For once, Julia did not feel the need to dive head first into the investigation. Maybe she was getting rusty or just desperate to enjoy what she could from the week ahead, but the call to explore did not come.

"You're cooking up a plan, aren't you?" Jessie

urged, shuffling to the edge of her seat with a grin. "Do you want me to take Honey? I can put the pressure on and get him to confess. He's only a twig. I could snap him with one hand."

Barker laughed, but Jessie shot him a look to let him know she was being serious. Barker disguised it as a cough and sat up straight, turning to Julia.

"A plan?" Barker asked, his voice wobbling. "I'm not used to being on this side of the fence, but it might be good material for the book."

Julia checked her watch and looked back at Honey and Russell as they counted through the money at one of the few empty tables. They appeared to be consoling each other, even if their movements felt a little acted. She assumed it was for the benefit of the room full of guests closely watching their every move as though waiting for the cracks to show or for the shock and hysteria to set in.

"A plan," Julia said with a nod as she pulled the napkin from her lap. "Do you have your phone handy, Alfie? See what time the first circus performance is at Blackpool Tower."

"The *circus?*" Jessie echoed, her face scrunching up. "What does that have to do with the drag queen getting bashed with the metal thing?"

"Absolutely nothing," Julia said as she stood up. "For once, we're going to keep our noses out and enjoy the holiday. What happened last night was none of our business, and it's going to stay that way."

"B-b-but-"

"You heard the woman," Barker said, clapping and joining Julia in standing. "The tower awaits!"

Proving that being almost eighteen did not necessarily mean constant maturity, Jessie regressed to her child-state and marched away from the table, her face twisted into a sulk.

"Teenagers, eh?" Alfie chuckled as he stood up to go after her. "We'll meet you outside after I've had a word with her."

Julia waited until Alfie was out of earshot to turn to Barker. Without him needing to say anything, she could tell he was sceptical of her reluctance to at least poke her nose in a little bit.

"Hanging up the investigator hat?" he asked, cocking his head as he folded his arms.

"I never said *that*," Julia replied, concealing her smile as she pushed her arm through his. "For now, at least, nothing is piquing my interest. We'll see."

"I can't say I agree," he whispered into her ear as they passed Russell and Honey. "I think you might have been onto something when you told me to write about killer drag queens."

IT TOOK LESS THAN A MINUTE FOR ALFIE to coax Jessie out of the B&B, and even less time for Jessie to apologise for storming off. Julia gladly accepted it and put it down to the excitement of the cabaret and the lack of sleep they had all got thanks to the police interviews lasting until the early hours.

As they walked along the promenade towards the tower, the sun beat down on them, promising to be another fine day. When they reached the base of the tower, Julia looked up to the top, glad of the cloudless sky.

"We'll be able to see for miles," Alfie said, pulling his wallet out of his jeans before hopping up the steps to the entrance of the red-brick building that wrapped around the base of the tower. "This one's on me. The new builder's yard has been treating me well."

After looking at the price list for entry to the tower and the attractions within it, Julia was glad she had not argued. It was triple what she had expected, not that she had visited anywhere like it before. Blackpool Tower may have been identical to the Eiffel Tower, but the closest Julia had got to that was spotting it in the distance during a dull coach trip to France during her school years.

With their wristbands applied, they were allowed into the bustle of the building. Packed with people hurrying in every direction, the entrance hall was much grander than Julia had expected. The Victorian influence was evident in the intricate red brick designs and the sweeping staircases on either side. A glance at the map on the wall informed her there was much more to do than a visit to the circus.

With the first show starting at one, they took a cramped lift up to the seventh floor where a new indoor 'Dino Mini Golf' course had been built. The thought of playing dinosaur-themed mini golf sounded unappealing to Julia, but after drawing in joint first place with Alfie, Julia found that she was quite taken with the prehistoric themed sport. With another two hours to spend before the circus, Alfie insisted they visit the Tower Ballroom, if only to look at it.

Julia had seen the famous ballroom on television many times before, but she had not anticipated its sheer scale. As they walked into the crowded ballroom, the vast expanse of the space took her breath away.

"How did they even fit this in here?" Barker asked, as he looked up at the distant murals on the decorative ceiling. "It's as big as an arena."

A mammoth dance floor filled with well-dressed waltzing couples dominated the room. Dozens of tables surrounded the dancers, but there were also two levels of balconies that seemed just as busy. Alfie directed them over to a table at the same moment a family vacated, leaving behind the remnants of afternoon tea. Once sat down, Julia took her time to scan the space, the vast amount of intricately carved gold demanding her attention. She attempted to count the number of crystal chandeliers and light fittings, but there were simply too many.

When a waiter cleared their table, they decided to order four lots of afternoon tea, which did not disappoint. Metal towers filled with sandwiches, scones, and cream cakes filled Julia up, the familiar sugary taste more familiar to her than the morning's fry-up. Just eating a cream cake made her want to immediately bake something, not that she had access to any kitchens.

In the middle of a spirited conversation about whether the ballroom resembled the one from *Cinderella* or *Beauty and the Beast* more, one of the dancing couples caught Julia's eye. The male looked instantly familiar to Julia, so much so that she almost dismissed it as a case of mistaken identity. When the couple waltzed by, the man's face in full view, Julia realised where she had seen him before.

"That's Tuna Turner," Julia said, pointing into the dancing crowd as he danced around the other side of the ballroom with his female partner. "I'm sure of it."

"The one who forced Barker into drag?" Jessie asked as she checked her phone. "The video is up to two thousand views. Oh, Barker. You're never living this down!"

Tuna, or rather the man underneath the character, whizzed by again, this time his eyes meeting Julia's. The drop of acknowledgement in his eyes let her know he was the Naomi Campbell beauty she had been captivated by during last night's show. She watched as he danced with his partner as the organist played a familiar sounding tune on the Wurlitzer organ on the grand stage. When the song came to an end, the couples stopped dancing while the people around the edges clapped. A handful of couples bowed and retired from the dance floor, but most stayed on. Julia was surprised when the dancer that had captivated her bid his partner goodbye and cut across the dance floor towards them.

"You were at the show last night," he said in a surprisingly deep voice as he wiped a glistening film of sweat from his forehead. "Sorry about dragging you up on stage. You were a good sport."

"It's all part of the experience," Barker said, his cheeks blushing slightly. "Just maybe pick on Alfie here next time. He was saying how he was *dying* to try on your lippie."

The man smiled, but his sadness was written all over his face. Julia shot Barker a 'be quiet' look as he seemed to have forgotten all about the performer currently strapped to machines to keep him alive.

"Tuna, isn't it?" Julia asked.

"Oh, yeah," he replied, almost embarrassed. "It's Marvin during the day. I like to keep the two personas separate. That's my job, although, after last night, I'm not sure what kind of job I'll have left at Sparkles. Russell gave us the evening off to figure out what to do after Simon's brains were half-mashed in. I haven't been able to dance here for months, so I called up one of my old partners. No use wasting the afternoon."

Julia noticed the sadness had vanished, and she swiftly realised his melancholy expression had been for the potential loss of his job and not for his colleague's health status. Suddenly, her interest was well and truly piqued.

"Have you heard how Simon is doing?" Julia coaxed, keeping her tone sweet. "We're all very worried about him."

"He's alive," Marvin stated, his hands planted on his narrow hips. "But he's hardly hanging on by the sounds of it."

"Must be awful to think of your friend like that," Julia said, feeling like she was about to push a button. "Such a tragic accident."

From the widening of Marvin's dazzling eyes as the next song began on the organ, Julia knew the button had well and truly been pressed.

"*Friends?*" he replied with a choked laugh.

"You've got the wrong end of the stick there, sweetheart. Me and that creature are nothing of the sort."

Julia felt as though she had poked a needle in the surface and struck oil on her first attempt. She tried to stop her intrigue from showing on her face, but she knew the corners of her lips were desperately trying to break free.

"Simon must have rubbed you the wrong way in the short time he's been working at the bar," Julia said, feeling Barker, Jessie, and Alfie's eyes trained on her as she attempted to pry more information from Marvin. "Wasn't Simone Phoenix new for the summer season?"

"I've known Simon for years," Marvin said before checking his watch. "Usually with drag queens, if they're bitter and nasty in drag, they're usually a little nicer out of it, but Simon and Simone are both dark to the core. I need to go. I promised Mum I'd drop by for lunch. She does her fried plantains on Saturdays, and I haven't had a weekend off in months. Simone has finally proven her use. If Russell figures out what he's doing, I might see you at the B&B again before you leave."

"I hope so," Julia said, more to herself than Marvin as he walked away. "I really hope so."

She turned back to her group, all three of them sharing the same 'I told you so' expression. Jessie had gone the extra mile and had leaned back in her chair, arms tight and lips pursed.

"I was merely making conversation," Julia said airily with a wave of her hands. "That's all."

"And finding your first motive for attempted murder in the process!" Jessie cried, her smirk breaking free. "I *knew* you couldn't resist."

Deciding not to take Jessie's bait, Julia rose and checked her watch, announcing they were going to be late for the circus.

"Just admit I was right, cake lady," Jessie whispered as they made their way out of the ballroom and towards the circus entrance. "Go on. Admit I was right about you not being able to keep your nose out."

"My nose is well and truly kept out," she whispered back, forcing a relaxed smile as she pulled the circus tickets from her handbag. "Now, let's enjoy the show."

Jessie snatched her ticket from Julia and headed to the drinks kiosk with Alfie, leaving Julia and Barker to search for their seats in the grand circus venue as it rapidly filled up.

"She *was* right," Barker said, his hand on the small of her back as they made their way down the steep steps to their row near the front. "Solving puzzles comes as naturally to you as baking."

"I know," Julia replied. "Just don't tell her that. I want to maintain the illusion that we're here for a nice holiday and nothing more."

Barker said no more. He took his seat and stared at her in an amused way. As Julia waited for Jessie and Alfie to return with the drinks, she pulled her small notepad and pen from her bag and scribbled down:

Marvin AKA Tuna Turner – Previous hostile relationship with Simon Blair AKA Simone Phoenix.

She quickly put it away, glad she had brought it on the off chance. For now, she intended to enjoy the circus.

CHAPTER 6

A fter a two-hour show of comedy, acrobatics, and a spectacular grand finale that saw the entire circus floor descend and fill with water, they left the tower in high spirits. Much to Jessie's delight, they agreed to save visiting the top of the tower for another day.

"Let's go in one of these amusement arcades," Jessie mumbled through a mouthful of pink candy floss as they walked along the promenade. "That one's themed like pirates. I have a bunch of coins burning a hole in my wallet."

"Are you sure they're not doubloons?" Alfie asked, elbowing Jessie in the ribs.

"What?"

"Pirate coins," he replied with a shake of his head. "Never mind, sis."

"I might head back to the room for a lie down." Julia rested her hand against her forehead. "I think I've had too much excitement for one day."

"You want to snoop without me," Jessie said, her eyes narrowing as she pushed a large piece of candy floss into her mouth. "You're transparent, cake lady."

"I'm just incredibly old and in need of a nap, as you like to keep reminding me."

"That too."

"Go without me," Julia said, stopping when they reached the amusement arcade that was indeed themed like a pirate castle complete with a large pirate skull. "I'll rest my eyes, and then we'll meet for dinner. I'll take us somewhere nice. My treat."

Alfie pushed his sister towards the amusement arcade and forced her through the door, not that

Jessie took her suspicious eyes away from Julia until the arcade swallowed her up.

"A *nap?*" Barker asked doubtfully as they set off to the B&B arm in arm. "Since when do you take afternoon naps?"

"Since I'm on holiday," Julia replied. "Enjoying myself is exhausting, and I barely got a wink last night."

The suggestion of sleep was powerful enough to make Julia yawn. Barker caught the yawn and fired it back, his jaw almost unhinging in the process.

"Maybe you're onto something," Barker said.

And as it turned out, Julia had been onto something. Barker fell asleep as soon as his head hit the pillow. As tempted as she was to follow through with her cover-story, she knew it was the perfect time of day to hopefully catch Russell. Leaving Barker fully clothed on the bed, Julia closed the curtains, draped a pink blanket across him, and crept out of the room.

As she suspected, the B&B was perfectly quiet. It was too late for lunch and too early for dinner, leaving the restaurant empty. She hovered around the reception desk, but Russell was nowhere to be seen. She considered ringing the doorbell but opted for knocking on the door to his drag den. She listened for signs of movement from within the room, but nothing came. She considered trying the handle but opted against it; they were not at that point of friendship just yet.

Leaving the drag den behind, she popped her head back into the restaurant. It was still empty. She knew it was very likely that Russell would be relaxing in his quarters and she wondered if the doorbell would summon him. Turning back to give it a try, the door to the cabaret bar caught her attention. Unlike on her arrival, there was no bingo calling or laughter drifting through. It was dark and empty, but that was not what had caught her attention. Even though there was a 'CLOSED' sign tacked to the glass, the door was ajar.

"It wouldn't hurt to have a look," Julia muttered to herself as she crept across the hallway.

The door creaked as she pushed on the wood. The hairs on her arms stood up, the air surprisingly cold despite the warm weather outside. When her eyes adjusted, she looked around the lifeless room, last night's music and merriment echoing around her mind like a ghost.

ICE CREAM AND INCIDENTS

As though someone was shining a lamp from above, a single slither of light broke through the curtains, casting a dusty glow on the stage. To Julia's surprise, the fallen triangular rig still hung down, its motionlessness a contrast to what she had seen it do.

Each floorboard squeaked as she approached the stage. Anyone else might have taken the creaks as a sign to turn back, but Julia pressed on. She justified her snooping by remembering that the police had not considered it an active crime scene.

Unsure of what she was looking for, Julia leaned against the stage and looked up at the ceiling. The rig had been attached to the ceiling by three steel wires, but only two of the wires were still connected to the steel structure. The third wire hung down, the frayed edge of metal jutting out in every direction. The half of the wire attached to the rig snaked across the stage with a similarly distressed edge.

Julia climbed the steps, eager for a closer look. She stepped past the abandoned Cyndi Lauper wig and walked to the other side of the stage. Standing under the hanging wire, she looked out at the empty bar, wondering what Simon must have felt like when he realised the rig was falling down on him. It had seemed to happen in slow motion, and yet too fast to act. Julia took pictures of the two ends of frayed wire on her phone. She had not expected to find a signed confession from someone who had somehow caused the rig to purposefully fall, but seeing the aftermath proved less eye-opening than she had hoped.

Resigned to the fact that it was probably an accident, she decided to join Barker while she still had time to take a short nap. She only managed one step before a distant shattering of glass made her spin around. It sounded as though it had come from somewhere behind the red velvet curtain.

"*Ow!*" a voice cried out.

Julia pulled back the weighted curtain, careful not to disrupt the rest of the lighting rig. She was surprised by how big the backstage area was. It was a similar size to the bar, but it was less elaborately decorated. A collection of tattered sofas angled towards a table filled the middle of the room, with dressing tables like the one in Russell's drag den lining the walls. It seemed to be where the queens got ready and waited for their turn to take the stage.

"Not the Barbra Streisand!" she heard the voice say from somewhere deep within the scattered racks of costumes cluttering the back of the room.

Julia walked around the sofas and towards the voice. As she had suspected, it belonged to Russell. He was sucking blood from one hand while he tried to pick up chunks of glass with the other. Russell looked up at her with a puzzled look.

"I was looking for you," Julia said quickly as she crouched to help him clear up the glass, which seemed to be from a figurine. "Butterfingers?"

"One of the girls dumped my glass Barbra Streisand in one of the boxes." Russell cradled Barbra's glass head in his palm. "They should have more respect for the icons."

"Was she worth a lot?"

"Not a penny," Russell said as he tossed the head into a nearby bin. "Found her in a fifty pence bin at a car boot in 2002, but she had sentimental value. I've had her almost as long as I've done drag."

"At least the real Barbra is still with us."

"Thank God for that," Russell replied with a chuckle. "I like you, dear. You're funny."

Russell found a dustpan and brush and swept up the remainder of the glass before tossing it all into the bin. The area behind the racks looked like it doubled as a changing room and a place for storage. Cardboard boxes with labels such as 'Summer 2012 Show', 'Royal Wedding Skit', and 'Wizard of Oz Number' were stacked on top of each other. After putting the dustpan back, Russell continued digging through swathes of fabric in a large box before pulling out a giant puppet.

"*Here* she is!" He proudly held up the fabric puppet, which bore a striking resemblance to Marilyn Monroe. "Reunited at last. I haven't seen her since the 2008 winter show. I bought this place in the spring of that year, but I quickly realised I wanted to host rather than perform. I cut my teeth with comedy in the clubs, so that's where I'm most comfortable. But, I suppose I need something to fill the extra slot or tonight's show will be too short."

"Tonight's show?" Julia asked as she followed Russell around the racks. "I didn't expect there to be one so soon."

"The show *must* go on, or so they say," Russell said with a sigh as he collapsed into one of the couches. "I've got a B&B full of guests. Nightly entertainment was promised. I can't afford to be dishing out refunds. We won't be able to do it in the bar, but there's always the restaurant. Some candles and free cocktails, and people won't notice the difference."

Sitting across from Russell, Julia decided it was not her place to talk him out of putting on a show. She turned her thoughts to what she had wanted to ask, not wanting their meeting to go to waste.

"I saw Marvin at the ballroom this afternoon," she started. "He's a great dancer."

"National champion," Russell said proudly. "Nobody can move like that boy."

Julia wondered how she could bring up Marvin's stern words about Simon without sounding like a gossip. She looked around the room while Russell brushed through Marilyn's blonde curls. Her eyes landed on a large framed picture of two drag queens on the wall above the row of vanity mirrors. Julia recognised the queens as being Lulu Suede and Tuna Turner. Russell noticed Julia staring and turned around.

"That was our first night in drag together," Russell said with a fond smile. "New Year's Eve 1999. We went to a huge Millennium party. I was convinced the world was going to end because of those Y2K conspiracy theories. We'd always wanted to try drag, so we thought we'd give it a go on our last night on Earth. We looked awful, and we would have looked even worse if Simon hadn't helped."

"You knew Simon back then?"

"We all met in a bar a couple of years earlier," Russell explained. "I was coming out of a dark place, and I was partying too much. I always ended up in this little basement bar down some backstreet. Simone Phoenix was the star attraction, even back then. One night, I was waiting for a taxi on the street corner when a group of guys mugged me. They beat me black and blue. I won't say what they called me, but they're words I wouldn't repeat in front of The Queen. I'll never forget looking up and seeing Cher's face. I thought I'd died and I was seeing the face of God, but it was just Simone. We went back to his flat, and he cleaned me up and let me sleep it off on his sofa. He tried to take me to A&E but I was having none of it. We were friends from that night on. We met Marvin not long after. He was in Blackpool for a dance competition and had snuck out to experience his first gay bar. I remember seeing this terrified kid sitting in a corner. I've always been the type to talk to anyone, so I walked right up to him, and he's never been able to shake me since."

"Marvin mentioned Simon earlier," Julia said, feeling her opportunity to dig. "He didn't seem too enthused about his old friend."

Russell laughed and shook his head as he sat the puppet on his lap. He glanced back at the photograph on the wall.

"See that arm around my shoulders in the picture?" he continued. "That's Simone. She used to be in that picture. Marvin brought it with him when he first came to Sparkles, but he'd already cut Simone off by then. After our first time in drag, we caught the bug. It's like a drug. You get to play dress up and bring out all those sides of your personality that you suppress the rest of the time. People assume you want to become a woman, but it's not about that for me. I love being a man, but I like being Lulu too. That wig goes on, and she takes over. It's fun! It's *art*! I get to escape myself for a couple of hours, and that's priceless.

"After the first time, Simone talked us into going professional. I didn't need much convincing, but Marvin did. He was big on the competitive dance circuit, not that he cared about competing. That was his mum. She was one of those pushy parents. He didn't want to let her down, so it was a blessing in disguise when he broke his knee during the 2000 Lancashire Dance final. He tripped on his ankle right before going into a split, and when I say that was a crack heard around the country, I'm not lying. When it healed, he couldn't dance to the competitive standard anymore. That's when he gave in to my nagging.

"We opened for Simone's celebrity illusion show. I did the stand-up comedy, Marvin lip-synced and danced, and Simone did her quick-change celebrity routine. It's what she's known for. Nearly thirty years in the game and it still impresses a crowd. Those were the glory days for me. We did that for two years, but Simon wanted to take Simone national. She became a touring queen for a while, so Marvin and I stayed behind. We had our own 'Lulu and Tuna' show for a while, but it was harder to get booked without Simone's name. Marvin ended up getting cast in a burlesque show, and I got stuck doing the graveyard shifts in half-empty clubs. I paid my bills with the makeovers at the makeup counters.

"When Sparkles by the Sea went up for sale in 2008, I begged, borrowed, and took out a mortgage that I don't think I'll ever pay off, but it was worth it. Not only did I have a drag home, but I could also give that to other queens too. Feather Duster pretty much came with the building, not that I'd ever dream of getting rid of her. She'll be here for as long as she wants to keep getting up and singing. There's not a person who doesn't adore Feather. She'll be the first in drag and the last to leave the bar. She loves entertaining people. They don't make them like her anymore. You're more likely to see Feather than Arthur, the man under it all."

"She's an amazing singer," Julia said. "It almost brought me to tears, but that could have been the piña coladas."

"Arthur was doing drag when it could still get you arrested," Russell said. "Feather Duster was a pioneer, so there was no doubt that she would be in my show. The queens come and go, but Feather is always there on time and ready to deliver. Marvin finally brought Tuna Turner here three years ago. I begged him for years. That's where the feud between Marvin and Simon comes from, although I didn't realise how bad it was until I brought Simon here. Simone ended up becoming the headliner at the burlesque show Marvin was part of. Marvin loved it and probably would have stayed there forever, but they fired him. He insists it was Simon's fault. He never really explained why, and I didn't realise how deep the hatred went. The club canned the burlesque show at the beginning of this year, so I swooped in and convinced Simon to do the show here. I sold it by saying he could do one summer and decide after that if he wanted to become a regular Sparkle Girl. I thought I was getting the old band back together, but it didn't work out like that. Simon wasn't the man I remembered, and Marvin can barely look at him. To say it put a wedge between Marvin and I would be an understatement. In fact, it's put distance between me and all the girls. Simone has managed to rub everyone the wrong way. Honey can't bear to be in the same room as Simone, or Simon for that matter. I had to give Honey a pay rise to convince her to stand at the side of the stage and help Simone with the quick-changes. That conversation almost caused World War Three. I wasn't going to risk asking Marvin to do it, and I'd never insult Feather by asking her to assist someone else."

ICE CREAM AND INCIDENTS

Julia soaked in everything Russell had revealed. By the sounds of it, Simon was not short on people who might have wanted to send a rig crashing down on his head. In the silence, Julia suddenly remembered the small interaction she had witnessed between Russell and Simon before she had asked for a hairdryer. Dressed as Dolly Parton, Simon had said a lot to Russell, but Julia specifically remembered him demanding a salary increase before storming off.

"What's your relationship like with Simon?" Julia asked, fully aware that Russell did not know what she had overheard. "Is there no friendship left?"

"There wasn't from the day he walked in here," he revealed with a sigh as he stood up. "I knew during the first ten minutes that I'd made a mistake. He was demanding things from the outset. That stupid lighting rig was *his* idea. He insisted on being properly lit, not that there was anything wrong with our old system." He picked up the Marilyn doll and set off towards the curtain. "I have so many calls to make. I need to phone the company who fitted the damn thing to tell them what happened. It's only been up for a month. The police want their information too. Feather thinks we could sue them for all they're worth, and the police have said they could be charged criminally, especially if – *if* Simon doesn't pull through."

They walked past the rig, the frayed edges of the steel wire calling to Julia. She had assumed the most likely explanation was wear and tear, but if the rig had only been fitted a month ago, it seemed impossible for it to have snapped so quickly.

When they reached the fish tank reception desk, Russell headed into his drag den, leaving Julia to run over everything she had heard. The background information on Marvin made him even more of a suspect, but the rest of the story also implicated Russell, and that made her feel uneasy.

Right before Julia set off back to her room, the front door opened, and Jessie and Alfie walked in, catching her red-handed.

"I thought you were having a nap?" Jessie called, dipping her head to lick at an ice cream cone. "Does she look asleep to you, Alfie?"

"I'm sleepwalking," Julia replied. "Where am I?"

"Hilarious, cake lady." Jessie rolled her eyes as she marched towards the restaurant. "I think it's very selfish that you're not letting me in on the fun."

Julia followed Alfie towards the lift, unsure what insight Jessie could offer. There was so little to work with. Julia had more questions than answers.

AGATHA FROST

CHAPTER 7

That night's performance had an uncomfortable undertone. None of the queens seemed committed to their routines, nor was the audience, which was less than half what it had been the night before. Lulu Suede's Marilyn Monroe puppet routine garnered a few chuckles, but the scattered applause at the end prevented an encore from happening. Feather Duster's singing was faultless, but Julia suspected the seasoned queen would put on a polished show come rain or shine. When the show ended, Julia was happy to be heading up to bed, the offer of free cocktails not enough to make her stick around.

After a shower, she thought she was ready to crawl into bed, but Russell's story would not stop whirring around in her mind. She sat writing at the table under the window long after Barker fell asleep. She wrote down everything Russell had told her as accurately as she could remember, as well as everything she could recollect from the events leading up to the rig falling. Forcing herself to write it down had conjured up details that had slipped her mind until they stared back at her. One of them being Barker's disappearance right before the rig fell, and another being that none of the queens had been in the bar either. A small part of her wanted to wake Barker to ask where Honey took him to clean up, but he looked too peaceful to disturb. When Julia finally let go of her pen, she had filled half her tiny notebook. She rubbed her hand and turned to the window, her stomach knotting when she saw the first hint of sunlight over the calm sea.

Standing up, Julia let out a yawn. She looked down at the notepad, but her mind was still running. She knew it was likely due to the exhaustion she was feeling from the pitiful amount of sleep she had got since arriving in Blackpool. She suddenly wished she could have taken that afternoon nap with Barker.

Her phone screen told her it was almost half past four in the morning. She groaned and plodded off to the bathroom. After splashing her face with cold water, she stared at her weary reflection. It would take more than the bright pink dressing gown to make her look alive. Yellow and purple shadows circled her eyes, and her skin had taken on a grey hue. She wanted to believe it was the harsh lighting above the mirror, but she knew it was more to do with her body not able to handle the lack of sleep like it had in her twenties.

She splashed her face again before dabbing it with a pink towel. A small part of her was disappointed when her reflection stayed unchanged. She went to open the door, but a muffled sound made her turn around. It sounded like someone was sniffing, or maybe even laughing. She stared at the white shower curtain and fear sprung up within her. She tried to put it down to her imagination, but she heard it again.

Reminding herself that she was almost forty and too old to be scared of the monster behind the curtain, she tore it back. There was nothing there.

"Maybe it's rats," she whispered, the sound of her own voice comforting her as her heart pounded in her chest.

She heard the noise again, and this time knew it wasn't sniffing or laughing; someone was crying. She stared at the vent in the wall above the shower, sure it had a similar placement in Jessie and Alfie's bathroom on the other side of the wall.

She kicked off her slippers and climbed onto the edge of her bathtub. Holding the curtain railing, she edged towards the fan, her ears pricked. She only needed to hear one more sniffle to know it was Alfie who was crying. Julia had heard Jessie crying, and this was not it.

"*Alfie?*" Julia whispered. "Alfie, can you hear me?"

The crying stopped, and she heard him inhale through his nose.

"Who's there?" he replied. "Hello?"

"It's Julia," she whispered, a little louder this

time. "Is everything okay?"

There was a pause followed by a deep cough as though an attempt to cover it up.

"I'm – I'm fine."

"Come to your door," Julia said. "Give me a second."

Julia let go of the rail, a decision she instantly knew was a mistake. Without the balance, gravity pulled her backwards. The shower curtain popped off one ring at a time as she fell bottom first into the tub. She landed with a thud, the curtain wrapping around her face. She did not move until she was sure she had not actually hurt anything, except for her dignity.

After scrambling out of the bathtub, which took more effort than she would have liked to admit, Julia assessed her reflection again. Her skin had turned from grey to bright red; it was somewhat of an improvement.

To her surprise, Barker had slept through her tumble. Leaving him snoring softly in bed, Julia eased open the door and slipped into the hallway. In a pair of cotton shorts and a white vest, Alfie paced back and forth in the dark, his neck to ankle tattoos making him look like a shadow.

"I heard you crying," Julia whispered as she folded her arms across her dressing gown. "What's wrong?"

"I -"

"Are you about to lie to me and tell me everything is fine, or that you weren't crying?"

"Yes," Alfie admitted with a sheepish smile. "How do you fancy watching the sunrise?"

WHEN ALFIE LED HER THROUGH THE FIRE escape at the bottom of the hallway, Julia's protests fell on deaf ears. He pulled her up an outdoor metal staircase to the roof of the B&B. Not content with being that high, Alfie climbed a ladder up onto a unit that looked like it housed the B&B's water tank.

"You're going to get us into trouble," Julia muttered as she clung onto the railing at the top of the staircase, the courtyard behind the B&B sinking away from her. "I feel dizzy."

"I came up here last night," Alfie called with a laugh. "Nobody is going to come up here, are they? *Come on*! The view is incredible."

With legs of jelly and feet of lead, Julia climbed

onto the roof. She had visions of it collapsing underneath her, but she pressed on to the ladder. She scurried up it, more out of fear than anything. After crawling across the top of the unit, Alfie grabbed her, and she sat on the edge, her feet dangling towards the tiled roof below. She was about to berate Alfie for being so reckless, but the view stole her words.

"Wow," was all she could manage.

"Told you."

Even though they were only a floor above their bedrooms, the view had transformed without the limitations of a window frame. The sea stretched for miles in each direction, looking as though it went on forever. With the usually busy promenade empty, it felt like they were the only two people in Blackpool.

"I woke up crying from a nightmare I was having," Alfie confessed after a period of silence. "About my parents."

Julia tried to think of how to reply, but the words did not come. Jessie and Alfie's parents had died in a car accident on their way back from a holiday almost eighteen years ago. Julia had read the details in an online article, something she had given little thought to while being in Blackpool, even though she knew she should have made the connection sooner.

"You're *from* here," Julia said, dropping her head and feeling like a fool. "Blackpool is where you were born. Oh, Alfie. I never connected the dots."

"It's not your fault," he said, nudging her with his shoulder. "I haven't been back here since they separated me from Jessie when they first took us into care. When I found out you were all coming to Blackpool, I was relieved I didn't have to come too. Dot thrust her ticket upon me. I didn't know how to turn it down."

Alfie had been so knowledgeable about Blackpool since their arrival, but Julia thought it had been because he had travelled the world.

"How have you found being back here?"

"Honestly?" Alfie asked, his eyes turning down as he attempted to smile. "Hard. It's been a struggle to hold it together, but it's helped having Jessie, and you and Barker."

"You've hidden it so well."

"You learn to," he said. "You have to, or you'll never get through a single day. Sometimes I feel guilty for having known them for ten years when Jessie has nothing, but other times, I'm jealous that she doesn't have to deal with the memories."

"Does she know the significance of Blackpool?"

"If she does, she's hiding it well," Alfie replied. "I haven't told her. She doesn't need that on her, especially with her birthday so close. She's becoming an adult. She doesn't need me dragging her back into the past."

Julia's heart broke for Alfie. She had developed maternal instincts for Jessie early in their relationship, but she had not known how she would feel towards Alfie when he first came into their lives. She had instantly liked him, but she had been wary about how to treat him. She had not wanted to overstep the mark, especially considering there was only eleven years between them. Staring at him as the yellow glow of the rising sun washed against his face, she could not help but feel the same protective bond she felt for Jessie.

"Tell me about them," Julia said, her voice soft. "What were they like?"

Alfie considered his reply as he watched the sun.

"Normal," he replied. "Really, really, normal. They were good people. Mum was a shopkeeper and Dad operated the Ferris wheel on the pier." He nodded to the giant wheel on Central Pier. "We lived in a little house just behind the theme park at the end of the promenade. It was a normal, three-bedroom terrace house. Nothing fancy. If that van hadn't crashed into us, Jessie and I would have been those people who said they had great childhoods. Instead, we were dragged through the mud. I'll never stop being grateful to you for saving Jessie. I know she can be a little brat, but she loves you. When it's just her and me, she calls you 'Mum' all the time. I don't think she realises she's doing it."

Julia fought to hold back the tears. Jessie had only called her 'mum' once before, and it had been right before she had passed out after being stabbed in the shoulder by a mad woman. That had been when Julia had asked if she could adopt Jessie.

"Being here doesn't have to be a sad experience," Julia said as she stared at the orange lines of the blurry sun as it peeped over the horizon. "It can be cathartic. I bet you never thought you would come back here, and here you are."

"I hadn't looked at it like that."

"And you're here with your sister," Julia continued. "And I *know* you thought you'd never find her after so many years apart. Dealing with the death of parents is hard. I was a similar age as you were when I lost my mother. I always miss her but walking in her footsteps in Peridale frees me. Do you want my unsolicited advice?"

Alfie nodded. Julia looked out at the sun as a cold chill swept past them, fluttering her hair across her face.

"Tell Jessie," she said. "Even if you wait until after her birthday, tell her. Let her in."

Alfie did not respond, but Julia knew her words had gone in. They stayed until long after the sun had fully risen. After climbing down and making her way back into the B&B, Julia was glad she had followed Alfie up to the roof. When she reached her door and tried the handle, she was less pleased that she had left her room without the key. Alfie pulled his out of his pocket and unlocked his door.

"You can have my bed if you want," Alfie offered. "I don't think I'll be able to get back to sleep anyway."

"It's alright," Julia said as she headed down the corridor to the lift. "I'll see if Russell is around. He might be up preparing breakfast. If not, I'll wake Barker up."

Julia went down to the restaurant. It was dark and empty, but she heard voices coming from the reception area. When she walked into the hallway, she saw that the door to Russell's drag den was wide open and that's where the voices were coming from. She had intended to walk right up and ask Russell for a key, but the tone of one of the voices coming from the room stopped her. From her position, she could see Marvin leaning against the dressing table, an almost empty bottle of wine in his hand. He was looking down at Russell, who was in his chair.

"In that case," Marvin said, pausing to glug the remainder of the wine, "you better hope he does die."

Julia gasped and took a step back. From the slur in Marvin's voice, she guessed he had stayed up all night to drink rather than having only just started.

"I don't see much way out if he pulls through," Russell said before sipping from his own drink. "He *will* come knocking for his money, even if he doesn't want to come back to work."

Marvin sighed and put the bottle of wine on the dressing table before crouching down so that Russell's face was level with his.

"Then I really hope he does die," Marvin

whispered, wobbling on the spot. "You don't deserve this. Simon did the same thing to me when he got me fired. You're a great person, Russell."

There was a moment of silence between them, and Julia took another step back, sensing what was coming next. Marvin leaned in and kissed Russell, but Russell wheeled back the chair just as quickly.

"What are you doing?" Russell snapped.

"I – I'm sorry," Marvin mumbled as he stood up and lifted a hand up to his face. "I'm drunk. I -"

"Yeah," Russell said quickly as he stood up. "You are. I – I need to – I need to go."

Russell walked so quickly out of the room that Julia had no time to make it look like she had not just seen what had happened. Russell's face reddened, and for a moment, Julia thought he was angry with her. He pulled the door closed behind him, his expression softening.

"Has something happened?" he asked with concern. "I don't mean to offend, dear, but you look awful."

"As do you," Julia replied with a smile. "You couldn't sleep either?"

"Not a wink."

"I locked myself out," Julia explained. "I left my room, and I forgot to take my key. Do you have a spare?"

"Sure, they're in -" Russell looked over his shoulder at the closed door as though a wild animal was locked inside.

"Starting breakfast?" Julia asked, the key the last thing on her mind now.

"I'm going to attempt to," Russell said as he walked around the fish tank and towards the restaurant. "It might not be my best effort, but I'll give it my best shot."

"I'll help," Julia said as she followed him. "I'm awake now, and I know a thing or two about cooking. Do you have cake ingredients?"

CHAPTER 8

Despite being exhausted, Julia did not mind helping Russell get the kitchen ready for the morning. She had hoped he would mention what she had overheard and seen, but he did not.

Even though she wanted to push the topic, she decided it would be best to wait until they were both better rested. A tiredness-fuelled argument was the last thing she wanted.

As it turned out, Russell had all the ingredients for a simple jam sponge cake. Even though it was a basic cake that Julia could have thrown together with a blindfold, the process of baking was enough to centre her. Julia slipped so deep into her own special world, she forgot she was miles away from home. For a brief moment, she felt like she was preparing for a day at the café. Remembering that it was Sunday was enough to pull her back, and also to remind her how tired she was. If it was like any other week, she would have been snug in bed and enjoying not having an alarm set.

Before the guests rushed down for their breakfast, they paused to drink large cups of extra strong coffee and enjoy the product of Julia's baking. The sponge was perfect, even by Julia's standards, and she enjoyed seeing the comforting fluttering of Russell's lids after he took his first bite.

Despite Russell insisting that Julia should get some sleep, she stuck around for the breakfast shift and helped Russell with the frying and stirring. She knew too many cooks could spoil the broth, but with them both sleep-deprived, she knew two tired cooks would be better than one.

ICE CREAM AND INCIDENTS

After popping out to the restaurant to let Barker know that she had not run away, she slipped out of the back of the kitchen and into the courtyard behind the B&B. Inhaling the warm morning air, she looked up at the metal fire escape. Her trip up to the roof with Alfie felt like a hazy dream, but his admissions had been too raw to be imagined.

Sitting on a set of stone steps next to a giant bin, Julia dialled the number for Peridale Manor on the B&B's phone. With her mobile phone in her bedroom, she was glad she had the number memorised. Her father answered instantly and passed her over to Katie, who had nothing to report about the café, other than that she was having the best time having a 'normal' job. Julia stopped herself from asking too many detailed questions, something she might have done if she had sensed anything other than joy in Katie's voice.

After the conversation ended, Julia dialled another number she had memorised due to the sheer number of times she had used it recently. A robotic voice reminded her that it was Sunday and therefore the social worker's office was closed, but they provided an emergency out-of-hours number. She called that one instead, but they were even less helpful than the usual people she spoke to. They promised to get someone to call back tomorrow when they had more information. Julia knew not to hold her breath for that happening.

After hanging up, she looked up at the clear blue sky and tried not to worry, even though Jessie's birthday was creeping ever nearer. She knew the adoption going through would not change anything about their relationship, but it was important to Jessie to have that official certificate to say that she had legal guardians, even if they would be redundant after her birthday.

"You look like you've got the weight of the world on your shoulders, poppet," a husky voice whispered from the other side of the courtyard. "Want to tell Arthur your troubles? They tell me I'm a good listener."

Julia looked across the courtyard to a door where Feather Duster, or rather, Arthur, was standing in a doorway. He was wearing a pair of baggy striped cotton pyjamas, a steaming mug cupped in his hands. His face was makeup free and his head bald.

"You don't happen to have any peppermint and

liquorice tea in there, do you?" Julia asked.

"Let me see what old Feather can do for you."

Arthur had been standing in the doorway to his own self-contained flat under the B&B, which he revealed had been his home for the past thirty years. The flat, which was modest in size, was decorated in a style Julia could only describe as organised chaos. The dark red walls were lined with an overwhelming number of framed pictures, some of them so old they were black and white. Julia realised they all had one common figure in each photograph: Feather Duster.

"I've worked with more queens than I've had hot dinners," Arthur said as he handed Julia a cup. "I only had peppermint tea and liquorice tea, so I threw both bags into the cup. Don't feel obligated to drink it, poppet. I'm more a PG Tips man myself."

Julia sniffed the steaming liquid before taking a small cautionary sip. It was not quite the same as the tea she adored at home, but it was a close imitation.

Arthur shuffled over to the couch and pulled off a blanket and two large pillows. He carefully folded the blanket with shaky hands, humming *Somewhere Over the Rainbow* as he worked.

"I've told that boy to tidy up after himself, but he

lives in his own world," Arthur said with a roll of his lined eyes. "But, Honey does what Honey wants."

Arthur chuckled as he motioned for Julia to sit on the newly tidied sofa. She did, the fabric old and worn but comfortable. The coffee table was filled with a stack of hardback books, the top titled *Making Faces* by Kevyn Aucoin.

"That's one of Honey's," Arthur said as he sat in an armchair swathed in multiple brightly coloured throws. "He called it the definitive guide to makeup. I had a flick through, but it's more for the young ones. I've been painting the same face for the past fifty years, and I'm afraid I'm a bit stuck in my ways, even if the canvas is a little droopier than it used to be."

"Honey lives with you?"

"I'm letting the boy sleep on my sofa until he lands on his feet," Arthur explained before sipping his tea. "I'm afraid he's not the first, and I doubt he'll be the last. His mother kicked him out."

"His mother?"

"Changed the locks behind him."

"That's awful."

"She could wrap her head around the sexuality thing, but not the drag," Arthur explained with a heavy sigh. "It's a sad state of affairs when a mother can abandon her child for wanting to artistically express themselves, but that's the way the dice rolls. It rolls that way a lot less than when I was Honey's age, but ignorance will always persist. Drag goes all the way back to Shakespearian times, and yet people still misunderstand it as something perverted and twisted. I'm seventy-five now, but I was twenty when I first discovered drag. Homosexuality could get you locked up back then, but that was part of the thrill of it. It was counter-culture. We knew we were risking everything for art, but I always find the best art comes when one takes a risk, don't you think? For Honey, I'm afraid five decades of social change means nothing when your own mother kicks you out."

"That's heart breaking."

"That's life," Arthur offered a slight shrug. "When you've been around the block as many times as I have, you've seen everything this world has to offer. The good and the bad. Sometimes, I think it's more weighed in the latter's favour, but I keep donning my wig, and I keep singing because it's the only thing that gets me through to the next day. I see that same fight in Honey. He's full of angst and rage.

When he learns to channel that into his art, he'll be unstoppable. I just hope he gets there before the cigarettes kill him."

Arthur motioned to a full ashtray on the table. Julia noticed that it was on top of a copy of Barker's book. She smiled but decided against mentioning that she knew the author.

"When you've been around as long as I, the pattern of excess emerges," Arthur continued after another sip of tea. "The drink, the drugs, the cigarettes. I don't touch any of it. Unfortunately, those three evils seem to go hand in hand with drag. Drag queens have been rejected by society for decades. Sometimes I wonder why we still press on, but then I remember how important our work is. We make people laugh and smile, and maybe we could do that without the wigs and outfits, but don't you think life needs a little razzle-dazzle to make it bearable? If people see us as jokes and not real people with real stories that we are, then I fear that's their loss.

"Nevertheless, I've spent thirty years as a Sparkle Girl trying to pass on that message, but it never seems to get through to the girls. They feel the rejection deep in their core. Some lash out, some turn to vices.

I've told Honey not to smoke in here, but the boy seems intent on disobeying every rule put in front of him. He could change the world if he just let himself."

"With a mentor like you, I'm sure he will."

"Me?" Arthur replied with a raspy chuckle. "I'm simply an old queen singing show tunes for a crowd that would rather me do the splits and a handstand."

"That's not true," Julia argued. "I was captivated by you during the show. You're a real talent."

"You're too kind." Arthur blushed as he readjusted the hem of his cotton shirt. "The trends come and go, but the classics persist. I noticed you in your vintage dress when you arrived. It put a smile on my face."

Julia smiled in return. People often questioned her love of vintage dresses with 1940s necklines, but they made Julia feel comfortable and safe. Subconsciously, she knew it was because her mother wore similar clothes, even if they had not been contemporary to her era either.

"I'm glad," Julia replied, pulling together her pink dressing gown and feeling anything but put-together at that moment. "It is rare people appreciate them."

"Well, I do." Arthur reached out and rested the cup on top of the stack of books before turning to Julia. "So, poppet. What has got you so down?"

Julia considered holding back, her problems feeling insignificant compared to the stories Arthur had shared. Knowing it might help to open up, she decided to tell him all about the adoption process and how she was running out of time to get the final official confirmation. Arthur listened with the concentration of someone who was being asked to memorise details for a quiz. When she was finished, she felt a little of the weight lift off her shoulders.

"I've had many children in my lifetime," Arthur confessed when Julia finally stopped talking. "None of them biological, and I never had any certificates either, but I've met countless 'Jessies'. Honey is one of them, even if I think he will be the death of me. You and I are the same. Kindred spirits, you might say. We see the downtrodden and the helpless, and we lift them up. It might not even feel like we're trying to do that or putting in much effort, but it's in our nature. It sounds like you're the best mother Jessie could have asked for given her tragic circumstances. If the adoption is legalised before her birthday, that's just icing on the cake. If she's truly become your daughter, you will both know that deep down in your heart of hearts, poppet."

Julia had said those same words to herself but hearing them from Arthur with such conviction and authority made her actually feel them to be true.

"She *is* my daughter," Julia said, her voice more forceful than she had intended. "You were right, Arthur. You are a good listener."

"It comes with age, poppet." Arthur forced himself out of his chair and shuffled across his flat to an antique dressing table. He picked up a hairbrush and handed it to Julia. "Might I prescribe a good brush, a bubble bath, and a nap. You're in Blackpool, after all. This isn't a time for heavy hearts and overthinking. It's a place for fun. The show *must*, and will, go on."

Arthur returned to the dressing table and passed Julia an ornate silver hand mirror. She brushed through her tangled curls, the soft bristles soothing. As she stared at her reflection, she wondered how Arthur had taken a word she had said seriously; she looked like a zombie.

Feeling grateful that Arthur had called to her

across the courtyard, Julia handed the brush and mirror back. The front door opened, and Julia turned to see Honey walking towards her. When he met her eyes, he paused as though he had just seen a predator about to hunt him. Julia offered a smile, but Honey did not return it. Knowing Honey's story, Julia felt like she understood him; Honey and Jessie had been cut from two ends of the same cloth.

"What have I told you about leaving the couch like that?" Arthur called as he settled back into his chair. "What time did you leave this morning?"

"Five," Honey muttered. "Six. I don't know. I couldn't sleep, so I went for a walk on the beach to clear my head."

"You didn't visit that mother of yours, did you?" Arthur asked with a shake of his head. "You know nothing good will come of that. In time, maybe, but not right now. It's all too fresh."

"I went for a walk on the beach, alright!" Honey snapped. "I need to get ready. Russell has asked me to do the ice cream brunch. He wants to see you too."

Honey pulled a cigarette out of a packet and lit it as he walked away, the door slamming behind him. Julia thanked Arthur for the tea and conversation before leaving him to get dressed.

She walked back into the kitchen, where Russell was leaning against the counter, his mobile phone resting against his chin as he stared into space. She pulled the hotel phone out of her pocket and placed it on the table, breaking Russell's gaze.

"Did you get through to who you wanted?" Russell asked, forcing a smile that was obviously for Julia's benefit. "You've been gone for a while."

"Arthur invited me in for tea. We had a lovely chat. Is everything okay? You look shaken."

Russell sighed as he tucked his phone into the pocket of his jeans. He turned to the sink and started to fill it with hot water before looking at the high stack of dirty plates and pans from breakfast.

"The hospital just called," Russell said, his voice shaking as he squirted washing up liquid into the water. "Simon's awake."

CHAPTER 9

J ulia resisted the urge to jump in the taxi with Russell and Arthur to visit Simon at the hospital. Instead, she went up to her room and passed out the moment she climbed under the covers. When Barker woke her up at three in the afternoon, opening her eyes felt like peeling back Velcro.

"You'll thank me later," Barker whispered as he pulled back the covers. "You won't rest tonight if you sleep the day away."

Barker drew back the curtains, the bright afternoon sun blinding her. Julia flung her legs over the side of the bed and forced herself into a sitting position. She looked down at the bed, and for a moment, she wondered where Mowgli was. The Liza mural reminded her where she was.

"We've been at the beach all day," Barker said as he applied sunscreen to his arms. "The weather has been lovely. Why don't you jump in the shower and we'll go back down? Jessie and Alfie are still there."

The shower helped awaken Julia's mind. By the time she was across the road and on the beach with Alfie and Jessie, she felt almost human again.

"We were just daring each other to run into the sea," Jessie said as Julia settled onto a beach towel next to them. "Alfie said he'll give me twenty quid if I do it."

"It looks freezing," Barker said. "And it's grey. We're still in England, Jessie."

"But twenty quid *is* twenty quid," Alfie said, wafting the note under Jessie's nose. "Go on. Are you chicken, sis?"

Jessie snatched the money from Alfie's hand,

peeled off her black hoodie, and sprinted towards the water in her T-shirt and jeans. She ran into the waves, the water splashing up onto her face. She let out a small shriek, her voice going higher than usual. When she made her way back, dripping from head to toe, it was obvious she was trying to hide her shivering.

"Don't call me a chicken," Jessie said through chattering teeth as she sat back on her beach towel. "Your turn."

"Not for a million quid," Alfie replied with a smirk as he leaned back to sunbathe. "You're too easily influenced, sis. You shouldn't let yourself be so easily coaxed."

Julia chuckled as she watched Jessie decide whether she was going to pounce on her brother or drag him into the sea. She did neither, instead choosing to expertly slide another twenty-pound note out of his wallet while his eyes were closed behind his sunglasses. The normalcy was almost enough to make Julia forget the events of the morning, which felt like a distant dream she had let slip away. When she remembered that Simon had woken up, she suddenly shot up.

"How's Simon?" Julia asked, craning her neck to

look back at the pink B&B. "Can he talk? Has he said anything?"

"I don't know," Barker admitted with a shrug before leaning back into his towel. "I haven't seen anyone around all day, apart from Honey, and he's not really the chatty type."

Julia leaned back onto her towel, but her mind was buzzing too hard to relax. She was desperate to hear the sequence of events from Simon's perspective, even though she knew she had no right to march into the hospital to question him. She looked back at the B&B again and wondered if Russell had managed to extract anything from him during his visit.

Just as Julia was concocting a plan to sneak back to the B&B to find Russell, dark clouds rolled across the bright sun. The sea breeze took on a bitter chill, making Jessie and Alfie both open their eyes. When Julia felt the first raindrop hit her on the nose, she sprang up and grabbed her towel.

"Typical!" Jessie cried as she scrambled to her feet, covering her wet clothes in sand. "Just *typical!*"

"British weather for you," Alfie exclaimed as he rolled up his towel. "You wouldn't get this on Bondi Beach."

ICE CREAM AND INCIDENTS

They ran back to the B&B, diving into the vestibule a fraction of a second before the heavens fully opened. Julia thanked Mother Nature's glorious timing as she unlocked the front door.

"I'm going to change," Jessie said, stomping down the hallway in her damp clothes.

"Did you take another twenty from my wallet?" Alfie cried as he flicked through the notes in his wallet. "*Oi!*"

Leaving Alfie to chase after Jessie, Julia set off towards Russell's drag den, but he emerged from the cabaret bar with a plastic bag at the same moment.

"How's Simon doing?" Julia asked quickly, the words tumbling out at breakneck speed. "Has he said anything yet?"

"He's said a lot," Russell said with a sigh. "He's making wild accusations too. I'm just on my way back there to drop off a change of clothes."

"Wild accusations?" Barker asked.

"Seems to think it was a conspiracy to sabotage his career." Russell rolled his eyes before looking down into the bag. "Part of me is wondering why I'm being decent enough to take him some of his stuff. Maybe I'm holding out hope that the bang to the head will knock out his nasty streak, not that it seems to have yet. The thought of facing him alone is putting me on edge. My nerves are shot, dear. I can't take another day of this!"

"I'll come with you," Julia cried, louder than she had intended. "I mean, if you don't want to go alone, I don't mind keeping you company."

As it turned out, Russell did not mind. He even seemed grateful for the company as they rode in the taxi to Blackpool Victoria Hospital, which was only ten minutes away from the seafront.

Simon was in a bed at the end of a busy row, his bed the only one separated by a curtain while the rest of the ward watched a property program about a couple who were desperate to leave the city and escape to the country. Simon being on a general ward looked like a sign of his recovery.

"Knock knock," Russell said airily with a wobbly smile as he peeled back the blue curtain. "Just little old me again."

The man in the bed looked up at Russell with very little interest. For a moment, Julia wondered if they were visiting someone else first. She stared at the bald man who had no distinguishable features and missing eyebrows. Was this the famous Simone Phoenix? Julia tried to conjure an image of the drag queen, but she could only see the celebrities he portrayed.

"I'm not talking to *you* until my lawyer is here," Simon croaked, the first hint of familiarity ringing a bell in Julia's memory.

"Oh, come on, dear," Russell said as he walked around the bed to pull up a chair. "I brought you fresh underwear and your shaving stuff. I know you don't like to let it grow. I would have brought grapes if you weren't nil by mouth."

Simon pouted and cocked his head in Julia's direction. He stared at her as though waiting for her to perform a magic trick. She offered a smile, to which he rolled his head to look out of the window. He exhaled heavily as though having guests was exhausting him. Julia wanted to tell him how lucky he was to be alive considering what had happened, but she held her tongue.

"I was in the front row at the show," she explained, walking to the bottom of the bed and into his peripheral vision. "I've been worrying about you. Everyone has."

"They have?" Simon asked, his voice lightening. "Well, it's to be expected. Most of the people were there to see me."

Russell shifted in his seat and shot Julia a look she knew meant 'can you believe him?'.

"Those flowers are beautiful," she said, nodding to the biggest bouquet of red roses she had ever seen. "Are those the ones from the B&B fundraiser?"

"Everyone donated," Russell explained to Simon, who seemed to be looking at the flowers for the first time. "I know how you love red roses."

Simon pursed his lips again and looked at the window. Julia racked her brain for the best tactic, a plan forming quickly.

"It was such a tragic accident," she said, repeating what she had heard countless times over the weekend. "Wrong place, wrong time."

"*Accident?*" Simon croaked, his voice cracking on its highest point. "This was *sabotage*, woman! Someone wanted me dead, but you can't kill Simone Phoenix that easily."

"Attempted murder?" Julia asked, edging closer to his bed, glad Simon had given her the reaction she had hoped for. "Who do you think would want to do that?"

"All of them!" Simon cried, nodding at Russell. "And I'm not excluding *you* from that list. Drag queens can be vicious. I should know. I've worked with some horrors in my time, and those Sparkles Girls were the worst of the worst. I should never have agreed to this gig. Look what they've done to me!"

Russell shifted in his seat again. In the silence, Julia heard a woman on the television exclaim that 'the cottage was exactly what she had dreamed about'. Sensing she had found her way in, she edged closer.

"I don't think it was an accident either," she whispered as she leaned her hands on the bottom of the bed. "How could it be?"

"That's what I've been saying!" he cried, his eyes engaging fully with Julia for the first time. "Did you see anything? You must have! You were front row."

"I didn't, but I thought maybe you had? You were looking in the direction of the side of the stage when it fell on you. Did you not see anyone there?"

Simon thought for a moment, seeming to slip back into the memory of being Cyndi Lauper. After an extended pause, he sighed and shook his head.

"The stage lights are so bright," he explained.

"You can't see anything. They blind you. It was just shadow."

"What about when you were backstage?" Julia probed. "Did you see any of the queens lingering between your changes?"

Simon thought again, his forehead scrunching, which was a peculiar sight without eyebrows. Julia suddenly realised he perhaps shaved them to draw them higher for drag.

"Honey was being a little brat as usual," Simon said, his eyes squinting. "He was going slow getting me dressed on purpose. I almost missed my Madonna cue, and I *never* miss my cues. The Freddie Mercury was supposed to be the last number, but I was debuting the live segment for the first time. After getting into the Freddie costume, I told Honey to go away. He was annoying me with that face. Always *sulking*! When I ran off stage to change into Cyndi, I don't think I saw anyone. In fact, I *know* nobody was there, or else they would have come when I tripped over that damn stepladder."

"Stepladder?" Julia asked.

"It was right in my path," Simon explained, his brow bone tensing hard over his eyes. "I tumbled over the thing."

"Was the stepladder there for the whole routine?" Julia asked.

Simon thought again, shaking his head more certainly than he had to any other question.

"I know it wasn't because it was *exactly* where Honey was supposed to be standing. That's why I ran into it. You get used to your marks."

Julia turned to Russell, who had been silent throughout their exchange. He looked uncomfortable and as though he regretted letting Julia tag along.

"Do you have a stepladder?" Julia asked him.

"Well, of course," he said with a forced laugh. "We use it for all sorts of stuff. It doesn't mean anything."

As though twigging onto what Julia was thinking, Simon's eyes widened.

"That's what *they* used!" Simon cried. "They put it there so they could send that thing crashing down on me at the exact moment it did."

"How many people knew about your new live segment?" Julia asked him.

"Everyone."

"He revealed it in the morning meeting," Russell

explained as he rubbed between his brows. "We have a drag family breakfast every Friday morning and talk about new ideas for the show."

"*Family?*" Simon echoed with a bitter laugh. "Those girls are *not* my family! One of them, or maybe *you*, did it." Simon lifted a shaky finger to point at Russell. "It's not like *you* weren't going to gain something from me not being able to perform."

Simon's bitter words made Russell jump up. Julia wondered if he was going to launch onto the bed to strangle the last bit of life out of the celebrity illusionist. Russell stepped forward and leaned over, his face level with Simon's.

"I had more to lose from all of this than I would have ever gained," Russell muttered through tight lips. "What happened to you, Simon? It's *me*. I would never hurt a hair on your head, but do you know what? Part of me feels like this is *exactly* what you deserved."

Russell slapped back the curtain and marched across the ward. Julia went to follow him, but Simon grabbed her hand, his skin cold and clammy.

"Don't trust him," Simon said, his gaze penetrating. "He's a good liar. He's trying to con me out of money. I don't know who you are, but you seem to be the only person speaking any sense since I woke up. Find out who did this to me."

Julia tried to pull her hand away, but Simon's grip was relentless. When he realised that he was hurting her, he let go, but not without squeezing tighter for a split second. Without saying a word, Julia chased after Russell, who was waiting at the top of the ward.

"Who are you, Julia?" Russell asked, his eyes searching hers. "What did you say you did for a job?"

"I didn't," she replied. "I just run a little café."

Russell did not look convinced, but he did not ask more questions. They walked in silence to the exit and waited for their taxi. As they drove back to the B&B in the rain, Julia felt like she was stuck between a rock and a hard place. She wanted so desperately to believe that Russell was innocent, but Simon's warning circled her brain.

"*Don't trust him*," he had said. "*He's a good liar.*"

CHAPTER 10

T he rain continued for the rest of Sunday and most of Monday, so Julia was surprised to see bright sunshine when she pulled back the curtains on Tuesday morning. Barker rolled over in bed, wincing at the light, despite them both getting their first early night since arriving in Blackpool.

Determined not to spend another day trapped in the B&B, Julia woke Jessie and Alfie for an early breakfast. After eating, they spent the morning with wax versions of celebrities at the Madame Tussauds museum before enjoying another lunch of fish and chips. With full bellies, they caught the tram down to North Pier on Alfie's recommendation.

"It was built in 1863," Alfie informed them as they jumped off the tram. "It was the first of the three piers. Started as just a promenade for the upper class to enjoy the views of the sea, but they got sick of ordinary tourists using it, so that's why the other two were built."

They walked around the arcade pavilion fronting the pier to the long stretch of wooden promenade that extended out into the sea. Unlike Central Pier's fairground, this was completely empty with nothing more than green lampposts and white iron benches running down the sides. Julia spotted a theatre and some other shops and cafes at the bottom.

"Where're the rides?" Jessie exclaimed. "There's nothing to do."

"It's relaxing," Barker said, inhaling the fresh sea air. "It's good to stretch your legs. Your knees will be creaking with the rest of us one day, so take advantage of your springy joints while you can."

ICE CREAM AND INCIDENTS

They set off down the promenade, the views of the sea around them truly stunning. It reminded Julia of the sprawling fields surrounding her cottage, the grass replaced with water.

They reached the end of the pier and decided to stop for a drink in one of the small cafés. Once inside, a familiar face caught Julia's eye.

"Fancy seeing you this far out," Arthur called from a table near a window looking over the sea. "I come here when I can to get away from the hustle and bustle of it all."

He closed the book he was reading and patted the cover. Julia was amused to see that it was a copy of Barker's book, which appeared to have been purchased from a charity shop.

"I've read that one," Julia said, concealing her smile. "Enjoying it?"

"I'm not sure," Arthur said, turning the book over in his hands. "What did you think? It's a little far-fetched for my tastes."

"I heard it's based on a true story."

"They always say that, poppet," Arthur said, tapping his nose. "It's how they suck us in. But, it's passing the afternoon while I drink my tea."

Arthur topped up his cup from a metal teapot with shaky hands. He motioned for Julia to join him. She looked across the café as Barker, Jessie, and Alfie looked through the menu. Deciding it would not hurt to sit for a moment, she accepted the offer.

"I heard you went to see Simon," Arthur started as he set the pot down before adding milk to his cup. "I hope he was in better spirits than when I visited."

"I'm afraid not."

"A leopard doesn't change its spots, I suppose." Arthur blew on the surface of his tea before taking a sip. "Did he have anything interesting to say?"

Julia thought about the stepladder as well as Simon's warning of not trusting Russell. She knew if anyone knew the truth about the Sparkle Girls, it would be Arthur.

"Simon told me that Russell owed him a lot of money," she whispered as she leaned in across the table. "He also told me that I shouldn't trust Russell. His exact words were 'he's a good liar'."

Arthur nodded his understanding as he took another sip. He set the cup down on the saucer and looped his fingers together on top of the book, his hands resting on the black and white photograph of

Barker on the back cover.

"All the best accusations have an element of truth in them," Arthur started. "It's what makes us believe them. He must have planted something in your head for you to bring it up now. Simon is good at that. He plants seeds under solid houses and cracks the foundations with the tree that grows."

"So, Russell *is* a liar?"

"He's a drag queen, poppet," Arthur said with a hearty chuckle. "It's his job to lie. He spends half his time playing a character, and when he's not playing dress up, he's playing another character, which takes even more skill. The Russell the world sees isn't the Russell I know. He lies to keep the peace, not to hurt."

Julia wondered what Russell could have been lying about. She thought back to having witnessed Simon and Russell's altercation before her makeover. It had only taken him seconds to apply an unfaltering smile after Simon stormed out of his drag den. She remembered thinking he was a good actor, which she supposed was the same thing as lying in that context.

"So, Russell does owe Simon money?"

Arthur picked up his cup and sipped his tea. He swirled the liquid around as he considered his reply.

Julia looked over at the other table where they were all watching her. She nodded that she would be over in a second before turning back to Arthur.

"Simon brought Simone Phoenix to Sparkles under the condition that he would be paid at the end of the season," Arthur said, each word sounding thought out. "Running a B&B in Blackpool isn't an easy job these days, especially one with such a particular niche. Twenty years ago, we had no trouble filling those rooms, but more and more chain hotels are popping up and suffocating us. Simone brought people back to Sparkles. I don't like him, but his name means something in drag circles. His act is a cheap party trick for the masses, but they lap it up. The truth is, Simone Phoenix doesn't exist because he's too busy being other people. Take away the celebrities, and I'm afraid you'd be left with very little. It's much harder to be yourself, don't you think?"

Julia nodded and recalled how blank and unrecognisable Simon had been during her visit. She imagined the blank canvas was a good foundation for creating so many spot-on illusions.

"Before Simon came, we were struggling to fill up to even half capacity, and the bar was quiet most nights," Arthur continued, setting the cup down again. "The winter season was tough. Fewer and fewer people come every year, which means the debt piles up. Russell is all about quality, and I admire that, but quality is expensive. That American diner cost a small fortune. He thought it would entice people in, but it rarely serves people who aren't already guests. When Simon agreed to work here for the summer, the plan was to use the extra income to pay off the most urgent debts, and then pay Simon a lump sum at the end. It was a good plan, and it would have worked, but Simon recently started to demand his money up front, as well as more on top. He's not stupid. He saw how full the bar was every night. He knew that was because of him. He wanted what he thought was a fair salary. I'd call it extortion. I don't know if Simon knows or even cares about the stress Russell has been under recently. He's a good man and he doesn't deserve anything less than the world. He just wants to make people happy, but I don't know how long that can continue. The chains have been trying to buy him out for years because of the size and location, but he's always resisted. One of the big hitters doubled their offer last month, and I know he's been agonising over it."

"Do you think he'd sell Sparkles?"

"I hope not," Arthur said solemnly. "It's my home, and I don't mean it's where I lay my head. It's where my heart is. Those silly queens are my family. Russell has said he'd look after me if he did sell, but I wouldn't want to burden him. If Sparkles closed, it would be the end of something bigger than me."

"Do the other queens know?"

"Not explicitly, but I wouldn't be surprised if they sensed something." Arthur locked his eyes on Julia. "I'd appreciate you *not* telling them."

"I won't breathe a word."

"Thank you."

"Is there nothing you can do to save it?"

"There's always something, poppet," Arthur exclaimed with a smile. "The show must go on, after all. Simone Phoenix isn't our saviour. There's always another way. If we can sue the company who fitted that rig, that would be a nice start. They took it away this morning to investigate further, which means we're back in the bar tonight. Can I count on you being front and centre for the show?"

"Absolutely."

"Then I shall see you tonight." Arthur stood up and picked up his book. "I need to go and pick out my costume. Russell has finally bumped me up from opening act to headline, so I need to make sure every sequin is sparkling."

Arthur tipped his head, tucked the book under his arm, and walked out of the café.

"Who was that?" Jessie asked when Julia joined them.

"Feather Duster," Julia said. "Or rather, Arthur. We were just talking about tonight's show. It sounds like it's going to be a good one."

"Did he have a copy of my book?" Barker asked, craning his neck to watch the old man shuffle down the pier. "You should have said. I would have signed it."

"He thought it was a little far-fetched," Julia said with a smile and a twinkle in her eye as she poured herself a cup of tea from the large pot in the middle of the table. "You can't win them all."

AS HAD BECOME ROUTINE, THEY BOUGHT ice cream cones on the walk back to the B&B. Through the windows of the cabaret bar, Julia spotted

Russell mopping the floor. She considered offering her help, but she decided against it. After their silent journey back from the hospital, she sensed her enquiring was starting to draw his attention.

Jessie and Alfie were not in the mood to rest in their rooms, so they headed in the direction of Houndshill Shopping Centre behind the tower. Julia considered heading up to have an afternoon nap, but as they walked past the B&B next door and she spotted someone biting into a slice of cake, the urge to bake took over.

Leaving Barker to go up to the room to work on his book idea, she continued walking along the promenade to a small corner shop. Once there, she bought all the ingredients for her double chocolate fudge cake and headed back to the B&B.

As suspected, the kitchen was empty, so she gathered the equipment and got to work on her cake. She measured out the ingredients, the familiar comfort washing over her. Baking had always been her safe place where she went when she needed to take stock. Being away from her café had meant she had been forced into a baking exile and it would take more than baking one jam sponge to ease her.

When the cake was in the oven, and she had whipped up the chocolate buttercream icing, she filled up the sink and started washing the utensils and mixing bowl. With her hands in the soapy water, her thoughts turned away from the cake and to her visit with Simon. The stepladder revelation had been playing on her mind, and she was certain that if the falling rig had not been an accident, the person behind it had almost certainly put the ladder there as part of their plan.

She imagined one of the queens standing on the ladder to somehow break the wire. The frayed edges had been too messy to have simply been cut, so she imagined it would have taken something like a saw to hack through it. The visual in her mind was so vivid, she could hear the metallic grinding of metal on metal echoing around her ears. When she realised it was not in her imagination and was coming from outside, she pulled her hands out of the water and grabbed a tea towel.

She pulled back the curtain in the back door, surprised to see Honey sawing through a piece of metal pipe. The saw made its way through the piece and the two halves clattered to the ground. After assessing the pieces, Honey selected one and walked over to what appeared to be a metal sculpture of a one-armed man. Honey pulled on a metal mask and welded the pipe to his shoulder.

"What do you think I should do?" a voice called from behind the bin out of Julia's view. "I can't live like this anymore."

"Are we *still* talking about this?" Honey cried, pulling up the mask as he stepped back to assess his work. "I'm trying to create art here. Just *tell* him! Everyone knows you're in love with Russell *except* Russell. What's the worst that can happen?"

Marvin stood up and came into view. He tossed a half-finished cigarette to the ground and walked towards the kitchen. Julia let go of the curtain and pressed against the wall. To her relief, Marvin walked right past her and through the kitchen without noticing the cake in the oven.

Julia pulled back the curtain again and watched as Honey picked up the leftover cigarette. He smoked it to the filter before picking up the saw to slice the remaining pipe in half again. Julia let the curtain fall down, her mind assembling the pieces of the jigsaw. It was far too easy to imagine Honey standing on a stepladder to cut through the lighting rig's wire.

CHAPTER 11

J ulia pulled her notepad out of her bag and scribbled 'From Julia' on a page. She tore it out and tucked it under the finished chocolate cake, which looked like it might have been one of her best.

With the kitchen clean and the only evidence that she had been there was the cake, she left, stopping in her tracks when she saw Marvin writing something at one of the diner tables. Julia turned back and cut a small slice of the cake and put it on a plate.

"Hungry?" Julia asked softly as she set the plate on the edge of the table. "I baked it myself."

"Huh?" Marvin grunted as he looked up from the letter he was writing. "Oh. Thank you. You made that?"

"I ambushed the kitchen." Julia hooked her thumb over her shoulder. "I hope Russell doesn't mind."

Marvin turned the letter over when Julia's eyes wandered down to it. She pushed the plate towards him, prompting him to take a bite. His lids fluttered the second the chocolate buttercream touched his lips.

"I've not met a man who can resist that cake," Julia said, pleased with the outcome. "Writing anything interesting?"

Marvin looked down at the letter as he licked the cream from his lips. He sighed and placed the cake back on the plate. Julia thought he might turn it around to let her see it, but he placed his hand on it.

"I have some things I need to get off my chest," he said, his eyes distant. "Some things can't be put off forever."

Julia tried not to smile, but she could not help it. Marvin's brows tensed as he looked at her, so she suppressed it, not wanting him to know that she had seen his attempted kiss or overheard his confession of love.

"The heart knows what it wants," she whispered as she patted him on the shoulder. "I'm sure that whatever you're writing will -"

Julia was cut off by the stomping of boots. She turned to see Jessie running across the diner to the lift, her hood over her face. She prodded the call button over and over before kicking the lift doors.

"*Jessie?*" Julia called, running across the diner to her. "What's wrong?"

Jessie looked up from under her hood. Tears were streaked down her red cheeks. Another set of footsteps appeared in the diner, this time belonging to Alfie. He looked out of breath as though he had been sprinting. When he spotted Julia, he took a step back.

The lift doors slid open and Jessie hurried inside, the doors closing before Julia could do anything.

"It felt like the right time to tell her," Alfie said, his hands on his head as he stared at the doors. "I thought she'd understand. What do I do?"

Julia pressed the call button and waited for the lift to travel back down to them.

"Let me talk to her," Julia said as she stepped inside. "You did the right thing."

When the lift made its way up to the third floor, Julia hurried down the hallway towards Jessie and Alfie's room.

"Leave me alone!" Jessie cried when Julia knocked. "Just go away!"

"It's Julia," she called back, her heart pounding in her chest. "Open the door, Jessie."

There was a moment of silence before the lock twisted and the door opened. Julia waited a moment before stepping inside. Like her own room, there was a mural on the wall, this one a still from Madonna's Vogue music video.

Jessie leaned against the headboard, her arms wrapped around her knees and her face hidden under her hood.

"Alfie just told me that this is where we're from," Jessie said, lifting her head up to look at Julia. "Or should I say he reminded me."

"You knew?" Julia asked, closing the door softly

before perching on the edge of Jessie's bed.

"Sort of." Jessie roughly wiped her tears away. "I've lived in so many places since then, but I vaguely knew this was where I was from. I heard the social workers mentioning this place a couple of times. I just – forgot. I was so busy living my life that I didn't connect the dots."

"Don't be angry with Alfie," Julia whispered, reaching out and resting her hand on Jessie's knee. "He's been struggling with being here. He didn't want to upset you."

"I'm not angry at *him*," Jessie snapped as she wiped her nose with her sleeve. "I'm angry with myself. How could I forget, Julia? I got so sucked into this life with you and Barker that it's just clouded everything else. My parents walked these streets and I didn't care enough to remember."

Julia shuffled along the bed and pulled Jessie in for a hug. She wanted to tell Jessie it was healthy to move on and that it was a good thing to live in the present, but she knew the words would fall on deaf ears. The seventeen-year-old had been through so much in her short life, Julia was not surprised she had overlooked where it all started.

There was a soft knock at the door, so Julia left Jessie to wipe the last of her tears to let Alfie in. He looked equally as devastated.

"Sis, I'm –"

"Don't apologise, you melon," Jessie cut in. "Is our house still here? I want to see it."

JULIA OFFERED TO STAY BEHIND TO GIVE the siblings some space, but Jessie insisted that she and Barker go with them. Leaving the B&B behind, they rode the tram a mile down the promenade, getting off at a stop outside South Pier. After crossing the road, they made their way to the Pleasure Beach theme park, its rides and rollercoasters towering over the busy roads surrounding it.

Nearly eighteen years might have passed since Alfie had last been there, but he led the way as though he walked the route every day. They walked past the theme park, crossed a bridge over a set of train tracks, and turned left down a path running along the tracks. They passed a couple of rows of houses before Alfie stopped behind a small metal fence. With the theme park directly behind them, they looked down the narrow street, fifteen or so houses on either side.

"This is it," Alfie said, exhaling heavily as he looked down the street. "Seaborne Avenue. It hasn't changed one bit."

They walked along the metal fence and through an opening onto the street. Small red-brick walls fronted each house, fencing off tiny gardens no bigger than the size of an average car. Grey bins stood in front of each house, hinting that it was rubbish collection day. If it were not for the distant screaming of the people on the rollercoasters behind them, it could have been any terraced street in any town in the country.

They followed Alfie down the middle of the road. He stopped halfway up and turned to number nine.

"This is it," he said, looking at Jessie. "This is where we lived."

There was a purple 'FOR SALE' board on a post in the small weed-filled garden. The windows were missing curtains, leaving a view through the small house to the overgrown garden behind it. Jessie approached the house, her fingers clasping around the metal garden gate. The woman next door at number eleven was taking her shopping bags from her car and into the house. She paused and eyed Jessie suspiciously. Julia joined her on the pavement and smiled at the woman.

"It's a nice street," Julia said, nodding at the estate agent's board. "Has it been empty for long?"

"Couple of months," the woman replied, her voice huskier than her appearance would suggest. "Polish couple lived there. They were alright. Quiet. Most people 'round here are, but you get the odd few. Thinking of moving here?"

Jessie unhooked the gate and walked across the weed-infested garden. She cupped her hands and stared through the window into the empty house.

"Something like that," Barker answered as he joined Julia on the pavement.

The woman eyed them up again before entering her house.

"I always wondered what it would be like," Jessie said. "I wondered if we were rich, or poor. I never imagined it would be so normal."

"We were normal," Alfie said, shielding his eyes from the sun to look at the rollercoasters at the bottom of the street. "We were a nice, normal family."

Jessie pulled herself away from the window and

left the garden. She looked up at the small house, and then to the outlines of the rides in the distance.

"I think I would have liked it here," Jessie announced. "But not as much as I like Peridale."

"I'll second that," Alfie said, wrapping his arm around Jessie's shoulder. "How do you feel?"

Jessie considered her response for a moment before looking at the house again.

"Like I've come full circle," she said before looking at Julia and Barker. "And that I'm exactly where I'm supposed to be in my life."

"You are," Alfie said, squeezing her.

"I don't even know what they looked like," Jessie said. "My parents, I mean. I know you told me, but I don't know for sure."

"I don't have any pictures either," Alfie said with a sad smile. "I've tried looking online but it was before social media was even a thing, and we had no other family to ask."

"Let's get out of here," Jessie said, pulling away from Alfie. "I'm glad we came here, but –"

Before Jessie could finish her sentence, the door to number eleven crashed open, and the woman from before reappeared holding a red-headed teenage boy by the neck. She threw him out before slamming the door behind her. The scene stunned Julia so much, it took her a moment to realise the teenager was Honey. She hurried forward and helped him up, but he brushed her off.

"What are you doing here?" he asked as he dusted dirt from his white T-shirt. "Did you follow me?"

"Don't be wet," Jessie cried. "I used to live here. What are *you* doing here?"

"I used to live here too," Honey said, looking back at the house. "Not that it counts for anything. I only came back to get the rest of my drag, but it looks like she's thrown it away. If she didn't want me in the house, she should lock the back door when she goes out."

Julia wanted to hug Honey, but she refrained. Honey did not know that Arthur had told her about his situation, and she did not want to reveal his story in the middle of the street.

"Let's get ice cream," Jessie exclaimed as she stuffed her hands into her hoody pocket. "You coming, Honey?"

"What?"

"You coming to get some ice cream?" Jessie

replied with a roll of her eyes. "We would have been neighbours, after all. I might have even liked you."

TO JULIA'S SURPRISE, HONEY OPENED UP about his troubles with his mother as they ate ice cream in a parlour he recommended. When he finished telling his story in his own words, Julia felt embarrassed for thinking of him as the prime suspect for trying to kill Simon. Even though the evidence stacked up, she did not want to believe the vulnerable boy could do such a thing, even though she knew it was still a possibility.

When they were finished, they walked back to the B&B, Jessie and Honey chatting like old friends ten steps ahead.

"That girl's resilience always surprises me," Barker whispered to Julia. "She bounces back no matter what is thrown at her."

Julia was about to agree, but two police cars parked outside the B&B silenced her. Honey left Jessie and ran inside, but they were not far behind him. Julia walked into the B&B just as three officers left Russell's drag den, one of them flipping a notepad shut.

"We'll be in touch," one of them said to him flatly. "I don't doubt we'll have more questions for you as more information comes to light."

Julia stepped to the side as the officers walked down the hallway. The door slammed behind them, sending a chilly silence through the B&B.

"What was that about?" Honey asked.

Russell, who looked like he had just seen a ghost, swallowed hard and leaned against the fish tank desk.

"The company who fitted the lighting rig suspects foul play," he said, the words almost choking him. "They're refusing to accept that it's wear and tear or a fault on their part. They called the police."

Honey looked as though he was going to say something, but instead, he ran through the diner and into the kitchen. Russell clung to the fish tank as though it was the only thing keeping him upright. Alfie and Jessie headed up to their room, and Julia nodded for Barker to follow. When she was alone with Russell, she rested her hand on his shoulder.

"Let's get you sat down," she said softly as she pulled him away from the desk. "C'mon. Into the drag den we go."

Russell let Julia lead him into his office. She sat him in the chair at his dressing table and looked around for a kettle or a bottle of water. Instead, her eyes landed on an envelope on the counter tucked under a makeup brush. 'Russell' was written on the front in curly handwriting.

"That's Marvin's writing," Russell said when he noticed the envelope too.

He pulled it out from under the brush and ripped it open. Julia's heart fluttered. She wondered if she should be there when he read it, but she was curious to see how he would react to Marvin professing his love. Russell scanned the letter, his brows tensing tighter with each line.

"It's his notice," Russell muttered, the words catching in his throat. "Marvin's quit. He's retiring Tuna Turner."

"Retiring?"

"He said he doesn't want to do drag anymore," Russell said as he scanned the letter again, the paper rustling as his hands shook. "He's done. He's had enough."

Julia wanted so desperately to tell Russell what she had overheard while baking the cake that morning, but it was not her place. Instead, she fetched the cake from the kitchen and handed Russell a fork.

"That's it," Russell said as he stabbed the fork into the cake. "I don't see how we can continue like this. Sparkles by the Sea is finished."

CHAPTER 12

The tension during the show later that evening was palpable. Lulu Suede's hosting barely extended beyond introducing the acts, and when it came to welcoming Tuna Turner to the stage, Lulu barely looked up from the laptop where her eyes stayed through the whole performance. It might have mattered more if the bar had contained more than a handful of people.

When Julia's eyes opened the next morning, she

was glad to be awake. She had been haunted by dreams of Tuna, Feather, Honey, and Lulu chasing her around the tangled corridors of the B&B. Each of them had been brandishing a saw and demanding their pound of flesh as punishment for her snooping. Julia feigned a headache and skipped breakfast.

Once alone in the room, she opened the curtains and sat at the table with her notepad. She looked at the sky above the sea. Grey clouds were hovering in the distance, promising more rain. The thick humidity hinted at something worse.

"Any closer to figuring it out?" Barker asked when he returned from breakfast.

Julia flicked through the reams of notes, but she felt no closer to cracking the case. She had settled on one of Honey's saws likely being used to cut the wire, but it did not make it a closed case.

"It could have been any of them," Julia said, planting her face in her hands. "They each have some kind of motive, but any of them could have put the stepladder there and cut the wire. I'm no closer to a conclusion than I was when it happened."

"That's not true," Barker said, holding his hand out for the notepad. "You now know for certain it wasn't an accident. Let me have a look."

Julia handed over the notepad and watched as Barker skimmed through the notes with more detail than she had expected. She had to remind herself he was a qualified detective inspector, even if she had beat him to the punch on more cases than he would have liked to admit.

"You're missing something really obvious." Barker tossed the pad back onto the table. "Alibis."

"None of the queens were in the bar," Julia said with a frown as she opened the pad. "That's obvious. I would have seen them."

"Yes, but you don't know *where* they were," Barker said with a smug nod. "Or, rather, you don't know where they *want* you to think they were. You could quite easily catch one of them out in a lie."

Barker was right, and she felt foolish for the oversight. She had been trying so hard to glean as much enjoyment from the holiday as possible that she had only kept one eye on the unfolding case. After she showered and dressed, she made her way down to the diner, leaving Barker to do some writing of his own in the room.

Despite Russell being at the reception desk, she

decided she wanted to speak to Arthur first. After sneaking through the kitchen, she hurried across the courtyard to his flat.

"Hello, poppet," Arthur said with a wide smile when he answered the door, still in his pyjamas. "Here for another cup of tea?"

"That would be lovely."

Arthur let Julia into his flat. She waited on the sofa, Honey's metal man sculpture watching over her from the corner.

"Honey has quite the talent," Arthur said when he shuffled in holding two cups. "I'm afraid I used the last liquorice bag on your last visit, so it's just peppermint today."

Julia accepted the cup and put it on the table next to Barker's book. From the bookmark, it looked like Arthur was reaching the conclusion.

"I might have judged it too quickly," he said when he noticed Julia looking. "It's rather caught my attention. You know, there's a woman in the book who reminds me of you. She wears dresses just like yours."

"Small world," Julia said, masking her smile.

They sipped their tea and chatted about the

humidity. Julia itched to start asking questions, but she liked Arthur and did not want him to think there was an ulterior motive behind her visit. When Arthur turned onto the topic of the police sniffing around the B&B, Julia shuffled forward in her seat.

"They've questioned all of us," Arthur said with a shake of his head. "I told them it was clearly an accident, but they seem to think it was cut with something. I think the company is worried we're going to sue them, so they're trying to wriggle out of it. Russell is in bits. We had a heart to heart last night. He's devastated. Marvin quitting is the cherry on top. It's his last show tonight. He's such a silly fool."

"Russell?"

"*Marvin*!" Arthur cried. "He's been in love with Russell since the day they met, but he's never had the guts to let him know. Seems to think Russell doesn't think about him in that way, but Russell just assumes nobody could love him because of the drag thing. They might not be kids, but they act like it sometimes. They're both their own worst enemies. Russell's too fixated on the idea that he's going to die old and alone like Hedy Lamarr with a telephone as his only friend. He can't see the sun because he's too fixated on the clouds."

"It would be a shame if Marvin left without telling Russell the truth."

"That it *would!*" Arthur cried. "I've wanted to tell Russell for years, but it's not my place, is it, poppet? Experience tells me you don't meddle in other people's love lives, but I'm not sure I can stand by and let Russell's great love slip through his fingers."

"Have you never had a great love?" Julia asked, her fascination about Arthur's life making her forget why she had visited him.

"*Me?*" Arthur laughed with a shake of his head. "No, poppet. My great love was, and still is, the stage! I'm afraid I'm a little expired now, but I won't die with any regrets." Arthur paused, his lined forehead scrunching up. "Actually, poppet, I take that back. I'll regret that I wasn't able to save this place for future generations. Spaces like this should be preserved, but Russell sounded quite sure that he was going to sell. I always imagined I'd drop dead in the middle of a Judy Garland number the way a drag queen should. It would be quite a fabulous end, wouldn't it, poppet? Instead, I'm probably going to move to one of those awful villages like in that book and take up chess or knitting and die peacefully in my bed. The thought is making my foot itch!"

"Little villages aren't so bad," Julia said. "I live in one. There's a cottage for sale across the lane from me if you find yourself without a home."

"I might take you up on that offer." Arthur chuckled before sipping his tea. "Especially if you bake more of those delicious chocolate cakes. I'm ashamed to admit I had more than my fair share, but if I am going to fade into a sleepy retirement, I might as well balloon up to the size of a house. I can't imagine there's much else to do at my age." Arthur put the tea on the table and leaned back in the chair. "If this really is the end for Sparkles, it's not just me I feel sorry for. It's Honey, and all the future queens like her. This place has always been a beacon for the abandoned and tossed aside, and without it, I worry more kids will turn to the streets and fall into those dark holes."

The mention of Honey reminded Julia of why she was there. She looked at the looming metal figure in the corner, its presence ghostly.

"Honey seems like a good kid," she started, choosing her words carefully. "I can't help but notice that he has some issues with anger."

"I worry about that too," Arthur said with a nod. "He lashes out a little too much, especially at people who are trying to help him, but I suppose that is the nature of a teenager."

"Do you think Honey would lash out at Simon if he had the chance?" Julia asked, her voice shaking at being so intrusive.

Arthur sighed. He reached out for his cup and finished his tea before settling back into his seat. Resting his hands on his stomach, he arched a brow at Julia, his expression making her feel like he was disappointed.

"Did Russell send you in here?" he asked, his tone shifting. "He asked me the same thing this morning, so I'll tell you what I told him and what I told the police. Honey did *not* tamper with that rig. We were both outside having a cigarette when we heard that thing fall down. If he did it, he has powers of telekinesis because he was right by my side."

Julia sipped her tea and waited for Arthur to ask her to leave, but it did not come. His expression softened as though he could sense her discomfort.

"I'm sorry, poppet," he said with a wave of his

hand. "It's just been a hard week. There's been a lot to come to terms with. The one thing I've been worrying about for years seems to be happening quicker than I would like, and there's not a lot left for me to do, and it's not for a lack of trying. Maybe time will show that Russell is doing the right thing. You wouldn't let a horse hobble around with a broken leg, so perhaps the humane thing is to put this old place out of its misery. You'll have to travel up for our final show whenever it is. I'm sure it will be one for the ages."

Julia promised that she would. She finished her tea and left Arthur to get ready to host that afternoon's ice cream brunch for the guests. She left his flat and walked back through the kitchen and into the diner where she was surprised to see Barker in one of the booths.

"It was too hot up there," he explained as he shut his journal. "I opened the window, but it made no difference. It felt like I was sitting in hot water. Attained any alibis yet?"

"Honey and Arthur were together smoking cigarettes outside," Julia said as she sat across from him. "How's the writing coming along? Going to share your idea yet?"

"In time." Barker closed his journal and slotted his pen over the front cover. "Honey and Marvin were in here earlier. I don't think they even noticed me come in. They were speaking quite candidly. Did you know Marvin is madly in love with Russell and that he's leaving the B&B because of it? Honey was trying to convince him to stay, but he said it would be Tuna's last performance tonight. He's getting a train down to London first thing in the morning to stay with some old friends while he figures out his next steps. They left about ten minutes ago. Honey didn't say where he was going, but Marvin said he was going to pack up his drag. I don't know where that is, but it might be a good time to ask him about his alibi."

Knowing exactly where he was, Julia left Barker to continue with his novel planning. She snuck past the open door of the drag den where Russell was talking on the phone. Once inside the empty bar, she climbed onto stage and slipped through the velvet curtain.

"Honey, is that you?" Marvin's head popped around the edge of the clothes railing at the other side of the room. "Oh. It's staff only back here, love. Are you looking for something?"

Marvin emerged from the changing and storage area with a dress made entirely of black feathers over his arm. He held it up before folding it and putting it in a suitcase.

"I was looking for you," Julia said. "Do you mind if I ask you something?"

Marvin folded his arms, but he nodded. Julia took that as an invitation to venture further into the grand dressing room. Marvin pulled a pink ostrich feather minidress from the rack and put it in the case.

"You have some beautiful gowns," Julia said. "I heard tonight was your last show."

"I don't know what I'm going to do with all of this." Marvin pulled out another dress and put it in the case. "Maybe I can sell it. There's no point clinging to Tuna Turner forever. I never really wanted to get into drag in the first place. I fell into it to impress someone. Sounds silly when I say it out loud."

"Russell?"

"How did you know that?"

"Russell told me how you met," Julia explained. "You were a competitive dancer, and he convinced you to become a professional drag queen after you injured your knee."

Marvin assessed Julia sceptically as he pulled out another gown.

"Regardless, it's time to let go," he said before closing the case and zipping it up. "I was never going to be one of the Feather Dusters of the world. I'm forty-two, so it feels like a good time to try something else."

"Change is good," Julia agreed. "I restarted my life again when I was thirty-five, and it was the best thing I ever did. My ex-husband kicked me out, so I moved back to my home village and bought a café. It all worked out, but I suspect that's because I was running towards something and not away."

"Are you suggesting I'm running away from Tuna?" Marvin asked with a shake of his head. "It's just wigs and dresses, love. I take the art seriously, but it's just that. It's not that deep to me."

"The drag might not be," Julia said, following Marvin as he walked around the rack, "but what about Russell? How will you feel when you live on the other side of the country?"

The question caught Marvin off-guard. He frowned at Julia before pulling more dresses from a cardboard box.

"I'll cope," Marvin said as he marched past her. "We spent years apart before I came here. As I said, it's time for a change."

Julia followed him again and watched as he stuffed the dresses into a black bag.

"I find it's easier to be honest when it comes to matters of the heart," Julia said calmly and carefully. "Everyone gets less hurt in the long run. I wish my ex had told me he'd fallen out of love with me before he replaced me with his secretary. I think Russell would appreciate you telling him the truth about how you feel about him before you run away."

Julia's comments visibly shocked Marvin. He stood completely still and stared blankly at her, his lips parted but silent.

"And *how* do I feel about Russell?" he asked with a forced laugh. "What do *you* know?"

"That you've been in love with him since you first met," Julia said calmly. "I overheard you talking to Honey about it this morning. I'm sorry, but I think you need to tell him. Even if he rejects you, at least you'll know. It's easier to fix a broken heart than a longing one."

Marvin looked as though he was trying to speak but the words appeared to jam in his throat. His lids fluttered, tears collecting along his lashes.

"Is that why you came looking for me?" Marvin snapped, his bottom lip wobbling. "To make me feel even worse than I already do?"

"It's the truth."

"It's *my* truth," Marvin cried, tearing his eyes away from Julia and marching over to the dressing table. "I don't see how it's any of *your* business."

Julia knew he was right. Perhaps she had overstepped her mark, but she rooted for love. The thought that Marvin would not give in to his would keep her up at night long after she left the B&B.

"I'm sorry," Julia said. "I didn't mean to upset you. I only came to ask you a simple question."

"What?" Marvin wiped his eyes and stared at Julia in the mirror as he gathered up his makeup.

"Where were you when the rig fell on Simon?" Julia asked. "I was in the audience, and I'm afraid the mystery of not knowing what happened to him is eating away at me."

"I was at a nightclub," Marvin replied quickly. "I used to stick around for the whole show, but since

Simon got here, I've got out of drag and out of Sparkles as quickly as possible. I only found out about what happened when Russell called me in the morning."

Julia considered asking Marvin what club he had gone to and if he could prove it, but she knew she had already said one too many things. Leaving him to continue packing, she walked through the curtain and back through the bar. She walked through to the hallway where Russell was scooping fish out of the tank and putting them in a mop bucket filled with water.

"The filter jammed up," he explained when he noticed Julia. "I thought I might as well clean it out while I'm here. It might take my mind off things. Can you imagine being so stressed that cleaning a fish tank is a distraction?"

"You've got a lot going on at the moment," Julia said as he scooped up the final fish. "Can we talk?"

Russell started the draining process for the tank before they walked into his drag den. Julia closed the door behind her, not wanting to risk their conversation being overheard.

She sat on the glittery, fabric-covered crates she

had sat on while watching Russell transform into Lulu on her first night in the B&B. Things had been so carefree and exactly how she had imagined a holiday in Blackpool would be. She could not believe how much had changed in that short time.

"I think by now you might have noticed that I'm somewhat invested in figuring out this mystery," Julia started, looping her fingers together and resting them on her knees. "I respect you enough to be honest with you, and I've grown to like this funny little place, so it breaks my heart to tell you that I do think one of the queens caused Simon to be hospitalised."

"And you don't think it was me?" Russell asked, his eyes locking with Julia's. "I could easily have done it too."

"Did you?"

Russell paused before shaking his head.

"Part of me wishes I did because knowing that it was one of the other queens is torturing me," Russell said, sighing and sinking into his chair. "I've asked them all to their faces, but nobody is admitting to it, which hurts even more. I thought we were a family. Family doesn't lie to each other."

"You'd be surprised," Julia replied, resting a hand

on his knee. "I've been lied to, and I've lied to my family when I've thought I was protecting them. It always came back to bite me, but it doesn't mean my intentions weren't good."

"And the intention behind hospitalising my star performer and the only chance we had to save this place?" Russell asked, his jaw tensing. "Our fate was sealed the moment that rig fell. I have surveyors coming tomorrow to make sure I'm going to get a fair price for this place. I'll need every penny I can get for when Simon sues the pants off me."

"Would he do that?"

"In a heartbeat."

It hurt Julia to know that someone Russell considered to be a friend could also be his downfall. Simon had not asked for the rig to hit him, but he had demanded money from Russell.

"What if we can prove it was one of your queens?" Julia asked, the question uneasy in her throat. "If someone is prosecuted, the blame will shift from you as a business."

"And throw one of my queens under the bus? They're my –"

"Family," Julia cut in. "I know. But you didn't

ask for this." Julia paused, remembering her reason for talking to him. "I've been gathering alibis from the queens, and I have everyone else's. For the sake of being complete, where were you when the rig fell?"

"I was in the bathroom," Russell answered immediately. "I was with Barker. He can vouch for –"

The ringing of the doorbell cut him off. Russell forced himself up and opened the door. As he passed the draining fish tank, the bell rang again, and loud knocks followed it.

"*Alright!*" he cried. "I'm coming, dear. Unless this is the end of the world, is there any need for –"

He opened the door and the three officers from yesterday filled the doorway.

"Russell Braithwaite?" one of them asked. "We'd like to ask you a few questions."

Russell sighed and turned around, motioning for them to follow him.

"Don't expect me to offer you tea," Russell said. "I don't see what else I can tell you that I didn't say yesterday."

"Not here," one of them called flatly. "We'd like you to accompany us down to the station."

Russell stopped in his tracks and stared at Julia with wide eyes before turning to the officers.

"Are you arresting me?"

"We'd appreciate your cooperation," one of them said, resting his hands on the handcuffs on his belt. "You can come willingly, or we can do this the hard way."

Russell turned back to Julia, the shock clear on his face. Julia wanted to intervene, but she knew anything she said would make the situation worse.

"Don't tell the queens," Russell mouthed as tears filled his eyes. "Please, Julia. Don't tell them."

Julia nodded that she would not as she watched Russell leave the B&B with the police. Barker appeared in the diner doorway, his journal tucked under his arm.

"Was that the police?" he asked, looking at the closed front door. "I just saw the car pull up."

"They've taken Russell," she said quickly, her mind whirring with information. "I'm running out of time. I need to…"

Julia's voice trailed off, something shiny and silver catching her attention in the bright pink stones at the bottom of the fish tank as the last of the water bubbled away. She picked up the net and scraped back the stones to reveal the jagged blade of a saw. More digging uncovered the handle.

"We need to call the police back," Barker said, his eyes widening when he noticed what Julia had found. "This proves –"

"Nothing," Julia said. "It only confirms what I already knew. It will make things worse for Russell if the police find this. Give me your shirt."

Barker reluctantly shrugged off his shirt, leaving him in a T-shirt. Julia wrapped it around her hand and pulled out the large saw that had been cleverly concealed in plain sight. Once out of the water, she wrapped the shirt around it and passed it to Barker.

"Take that up to our room," Julia ordered. "We're going to need it later."

"*Later?*" Barker replied with a confused laugh. "Have you lost your mind? What's happening later?"

Julia blinked hard as a plan formed in her mind. She knew there was only one way she was going to unravel the case once and for all.

"The show," Julia said as she looked down into the mop bucket full of fish. "We're going to confront the queens and get the truth out of them. Until then, we carry on as normal. The show must go on. We don't tell anyone where Russell is or about what we found. Promise, Barker?"

AGATHA FROST

CHAPTER 13

Rain drizzled down the window as Julia put in her diamond earrings in front of the dressing table mirror. A crack of purple lightning cut across the dark sky, lighting up the dark waves below. The following rumble of thunder made Julia jump and drop the back of her earring.

"I have a bad feeling about this," Barker muttered as he tweaked the curtains. "Are you sure you want to get involved in this mess?"

Julia dropped to her knees and felt under the bed for the fallen piece. Her eyes levelled with the shirt bundle on the bed.

"I'm sure," Julia replied, her fingers closing around the earring back. "It's the only way."

Barker huffed as he closed the curtains. He had been trying to convince her it was not the only way, but Julia's mind was made up. She secured the earring and brushed down the creases in her flared black dress; the colour felt fitting for the situation.

They met Jessie and Alfie in the hallway at the agreed time and made their way down to the bar. Julia wanted to be right at the front, not that they had much competition for getting a table. When Feather Duster shuffled out with a microphone and climbed into the DJ booth, the bar was the emptiest she had seen it.

Feather's opening monologue proved that she was as good a comedienne as she was a singer, even if the laughter was scattered. Honey opened the show with an energetic dance routine, followed by Tuna, who had chosen to repeat her Shania Twain routine for her last performance. After quickly dressing another uncomfortable man in drag, she left the stage without as much of a bow. When it came time for Feather to get up and sing, Julia was glad of the change of mood. As usual, Feather's singing was faultless as she worked her way through the *Wicked* soundtrack, finishing with a rousing rendition of *Defying Gravity*. When she reached the final note, Feather's eyes filled with tears, as did Julia's. Julia saw through the drag and sensed Arthur's heartbreak at the end of an era coming quickly.

When the show ended, Julia looked down at the shirt-covered saw poking out of her handbag; she knew the time had come.

"What're we doing now?" Jessie asked. "Why don't we go to a club? Honey told me there were loads further into town."

"You're still seventeen for two more days," Alfie reminded her before pinching her cheek. "Tough luck."

"*One* more day," Jessie said after checking her watch. "It's past midnight, so the joke's on you. Nobody is even going to notice."

Julia looked at the curtain, knowing time was slipping away from her. Barker caught her eye and shrugged as though asking what she was going to do.

"I need the loo," Julia said, picking up her bag as she stood up. "Decide what we're going to do before I get back."

Julia left the table and walked towards the door. When Jessie and Alfie reignited their squabble, she detoured towards the stage, glad that Feather had turned the lights off. Taking a deep breath, Julia slipped through the curtain.

"Selling?" Honey cried. "What do you mean Russell is selling the B&B? Where is he anyway? That man doesn't take nights off."

"He's selling to one of the chains," Marvin said as he peeled off his Tuna Turner wig in the mirror. "It's probably for the best. I don't see how he's going to come back from this, especially now that Simon's awake."

"Ladies," Arthur said, his wig in his lap as he removed his makeup with a wipe on one of the couches. "We have company."

Julia hid the bag behind her back and took a step into the room. Marvin glared at her through the mirror as he wiped away Tuna Turner for the last time. She could tell she was not forgiven for her comments to him that afternoon. Honey pulled off his wig and leaned against the couch behind Arthur before scrolling through his phone.

"You know you're not allowed back here," Marvin said quietly as he assessed his clean face in the mirror. "But, something tells me you don't care about that."

"She's alright," Honey said with a shrug. "She bought me ice cream."

"You're too easily bought." Marvin screwed up his makeup wipes before strutting off to the changing area behind the racks at the back of the room.

Julia stood in the awkward silence as Arthur and Honey watched and waited for her to speak. She stepped forward and cleared her throat, but the words would not come. Instead, she pulled the shirt bundle out of her bag and unwrapped it. With the fabric still around the handle, she held it up.

"Does this look familiar to -"

"What's going on?" a voice from behind cut her off. "Julia? What are you doing?"

Julia turned, surprised to see Russell, his hair and clothes thoroughly soaked. Thunder rumbled in the distance, sending a shiver down Julia's spine.

"Where've you been?" Honey asked, pushing his phone into his costume before jumping over the couch to sit next to Arthur. "Is it true you're selling this place? Is that one of my saws? Where did you get that?"

Julia looked at the saw, its presence not having the impact she had expected. Marvin returned from the changing area out of his costume and heels and into a simple black shirt with jeans. His eyes widened when he saw Russell, but they did not react when they noticed the saw.

"Julia?" Russell asked again, searching her eyes for an explanation. "Where did you get that?"

"I found it in your fish tank," Julia said, another deep growl of thunder rumbling the building. "How did you get out?"

"Get out?" Arthur echoed as he wiped off the last of his lipstick. "I thought you were having the night off?"

"I thought you were avoiding me," Marvin said as he perched on the edge of the couch next to Arthur.

"The police wanted to talk to me," Russell explained carefully, his eyes still on Julia. "I asked her not to say anything because I didn't want to ruin

Marvin's last show. With the lighting company calling the police, they are suddenly taking Simon's accusations seriously. He seems convinced I was the one who caused it."

"Oh, get real!" Honey cried with a roll of his eyes that reminded Julia of Jessie. "I thought it was an accident? Did you say you found that saw in the fish tank? I thought I'd lost it. I haven't seen it since –"

"Friday?" Julia cut in. "That's my guess."

"Well, yeah," Honey replied. "What of it?"

"Considering that someone buried this in the stones in the tank tells me they didn't want anyone to find it," Julia continued, her voice strengthening. "It was a good place to hide it, if only temporarily. If it weren't for the filter jamming up, I would never have noticed it shining through. Of course, this doesn't really matter, does it? One of you knows you're lying about your alibi."

"Is this woman for real?" Marvin laughed as he looked around the room. "You're not taking this seriously, are you?"

Julia tossed the saw onto the coffee table. It broke free of the shirt and clattered against the wood. The trio on the couches stared at it before looking up at

Julia.

"Russell spent the day at the police station," Julia continued. "I lied for him earlier because I wanted to make sure you were all here tonight. This isn't going away. If one of you doesn't admit to it, then -"

Before Julia could finish her sentence, Russell pulled her back through the curtains to the shadowy side of the stage. The bar had almost emptied with her table the only one with people still sitting. She looked up at the cut wire above their heads.

"What are you doing?" he whispered darkly. "I told you, I'm not throwing them under the bus. It's not fair."

"And the police arresting you is?" Julia replied. "You can't sacrifice yourself for them, no matter how much you care about them."

"Why can't I?" Russell snapped, his eyes unblinking. "What do I have to live for, Julia? I'm a forty-two-year-old drag queen up to my eyeballs in debt. When this place is gone, I'll have nothing left. If I ride this out, the police will give up eventually. They have no evidence, or they wouldn't have released me."

"And what about Simon?" Julia asked after

exhaling. "Do you think he's going to give up? You might not like him – heck, I don't even like him, and I barely know him – but someone tried to murder him. Do you think that's fair?"

Russell went to reply but he stopped himself. He sighed and rubbed the lines on his forehead before shaking his head.

"I should never have offered those tickets for that damn fête," Russell replied with a sad smile. "Some woman called Amy kept harassing me over email for them. I only agreed because we were two rooms away from being full for the first time in years. You're not going to let this drop, are you?"

"Do you want me to?" Julia asked as she searched his eyes for the answer. "I can go up to my room, pack my bag, and be home before the sun rises. If that's what you want, say the word, but you and I both know that your problems aren't going to go away just because I do."

Russell went to reply but the curtain opened, and Marvin walked through, headphones over his ears. He jumped off the stage and headed for the door.

"He's probably going to a club," Russell explained. "He spends most nights there now. I don't know what's happened to him."

"He's got a lot on his mind," Julia said, the words leaving her mouth before she realised she was saying them. "It's none of my business. None of this is."

"What's on his mind?"

"You'll have to ask him," Julia said, her eyes darting to the floor. "I can see I'm not getting anywhere here. I'm sorry for sticking my nose in. Some people back home say I can't help myself, and they're probably right. This time, I'm stepping away and throwing my hands up in defeat. I haven't figured it out and no one is about to start telling the truth any time soon. The saw is in there. Do what you want with it."

"You're not going to call the police?"

"Not this time," Julia replied as she patted him on the shoulder. "I really wish it had been an accident."

Leaving Russell in the shadows, she climbed off the stage and walked over to the table. Jessie and Alfie were both on their phones, but Barker's eyes were trained on her.

"Well?" he asked. "What happened?"

"She went to the bog," Jessie cried with a roll of

her eyes. "And she was gone for ten minutes. What do you *think* happened?"

Julia could not help but smile. She looked around the empty and silent bar as the bartenders collected the last of the glasses; she had never felt further from home.

"Should we go home?" Julia asked as she sat back down. "I miss Peridale."

"Me too," Jessie said.

"Me three," Barker replied.

"I'll drink to that," Alfie said, lifting his pint before finishing the rest of the lager. "Being here has made me realise where my home really is."

They left the bar and agreed to pack as quickly as they could. Julia thought she would feel disappointed at not reaching a solid conclusion, but as she sat next to her packed case and stared at the Liza mural, she felt strangely content.

"Sometimes the dice rolls this way," Barker said as he zipped up his case. "I never solved every case I worked on. You learn to live with it."

"Simon is alive," Julia said, standing up and dragging her case off the bed. "That's the most important thing, I suppose."

"I'm proud of you." Barker kissed her and pulled her into a hug. "It's not easy admitting defeat."

"We got a nice break out of it."

"We did," Barker said as he pulled away. "Although, I'll be glad not to have Liza Minelli gawking at me every night. I can't tell you how many times I've woken up in the middle of the night and almost had a heart attack."

They took their bags into the hallway where Jessie and Alfie were already waiting for them. Even though it felt strange to be leaving in the middle of the night, it felt like the right thing to do. As they walked to the lift, Julia and Barker agreed to split the driving between them, despite Jessie's offer to drive.

"So, who do you think tried to kill Simon?" Jessie asked as the lift made its way down to the ground floor. "You *must* have a hunch, cake lady."

"It doesn't matter," Julia said, pulling Jessie into her side. "This one isn't for us, kid."

"But who do you *think* did it?" Jessie pouted. "Spill!"

Julia chuckled, but she shook her head. The truth was, she was not sure. Like Arthur had said, drag queens were great actors. She could usually detect when someone was lying, but she had believed all their alibis. If someone confessed one day, it would be nice to hear about it, but she was not going to lose any sleep over the loose ends.

Julia left their room keys on the counter. Even though she could see Russell through a crack in the open drag den door, she decided not to say goodbye; there was nothing left to say. When the front door closed behind them, she felt a slight tinge of sadness that their holiday had been tainted by something out of their control. If they had enjoyed a week of shows like the first night, she might have been leaving Blackpool in higher spirits.

"I'll be glad to have my own bed again," Jessie called as they hurried down the dark street in the rain. "And I miss Mowgli scratching me to wake me up."

"I miss the same about Dot," Alfie called back. "Although she doesn't scratch, she just screams up the stairs and hits a pan with a wooden spoon until I get out of bed."

They made their way around the corner and Julia's precious car came into view. Peridale was calling, and she was ready to answer. Jessie missed her bed and Alfie missed Dot, but Julia missed her café;

she hoped Katie would not mind handing the keys back a day early.

Once they were at the car, Julia dug in her bag for the keys. Her fingers closed around the cold metal. She pulled them out, her notepad coming with them. It landed on the wet road, the rain instantly making the ink bleed. She immediately recognised the alibi notes. As she picked it up, one word caught her attention.

"Cigarettes," she mumbled to herself. "They were smoking cigarettes."

"*Huh?*" Jessie called. "C'mon, cake lady! I'm soaked!"

Julia stuffed the notepad back in her bag and unlocked the boot. Once their cases were inside, Julia unlocked the other doors, but she paused before climbing inside.

"I think I've left my phone in the room," Julia called into the car as the other three were fastening their seatbelts. "Wait here. I'll be two minutes."

Julia did not wait for a reply. She set off back towards the B&B, the pieces finally slotting into place.

ICE CREAM AND INCIDENTS

JULIA SNUCK IN BEHIND TWO GUESTS who smelled like they were returning from a night at the pub. She was glad she had not needed to ring the doorbell. She sidled past the reception, Russell still visible from his drag den. She made her way through the kitchen and tried to open the back door; it was locked. She looked around the kitchen for the key, but it was nowhere in sight. She almost admitted defeat until she remembered something Alfie had shown her.

Julia took the lift up to the first floor. Just like the third floor, there was a fire door at the end of the corridor. She carefully pushed open the door and climbed onto the metal staircase. A purple streak of lightning cracked through the darkness. She gripped tightly to the wet handrail, her knees knocking together. After taking a deep breath, she carefully made her way down to the courtyard.

As she ran to Arthur's flat, more lightning illuminated her path, not that she needed it; his lights were on. Julia knocked softly on the door, not wanting to cause any alarm.

The door opened a crack and Arthur peered

through the chain.

"Can I come in?" Julia called over the rain. "I'm a little wet here."

Arthur stared at her and frowned. He closed the door, rattled the chain, and let her in.

"I'm a little busy," Arthur said as he hurried into his sitting room. "What is it, Julia?"

Half of the pictures that had covered the walls on her first visit were now down and in a box. He reached up and grabbed another, his fingers running across the glass as he packed it away.

"Is Honey here?" Julia asked, pushing her damp hair from her eyes. "I wanted to ask him something."

"He's gone out with Marvin," Arthur said as he gathered up more pictures and put them in the box on the coffee table. "Let the kid enjoy his last night with his friend. If that's all, I really am quite busy. I don't have much time to get this –"

"You told me you hated smoking," Julia interrupted, not needing to pull out her notepad to recite the fact. "You said you didn't touch the things."

"Yes?" Arthur snapped. "That's true."

"I don't disbelieve you."

"Well, what does that have to do with anything,

poppet? I really do need to get on with this."

"It's only just clicked," Julia said. "You lied about your alibi. You told me you were smoking with Honey when the rig fell."

"Did I?" Arthur replied quickly with a wave of his hand. "I'm sure I said I was with Honey and *he* was smoking."

"Your exact words were 'we were both outside having a cigarette'." Julia reached into her handbag and pulled out the sodden notepad. "It's bled, but you can still read it. I wrote it down word for word."

Arthur glanced at the running ink before returning to his picture gathering.

"I'm an old man, poppet. I can't remember what I did and didn't say. We were smoking, he was smoking – what's the difference? We were together."

"Because one is a lie," Julia said softly. "And it means you're either covering for Honey, or you're covering for yourself, except Honey was quite surprised when I pulled out that saw."

Arthur looked over his shoulder at Julia, his hands firmly gripping a photo frame. He looked down at it, a fond smile shaking his lips.

"We were a family," Arthur said as he showed

Julia the photograph. "Dysfunctional, but happy. You're right. It was me."

Arthur collapsed into his armchair, the photograph clutched to his chest. He closed his eyes and sighed. The confession seemed to have taken his last ounce of energy.

"I wish I was wrong," Julia said as she perched on the edge of the couch. "I was about to go home, but my notepad fell out. I should have just left it."

"Bless you, poppet," Arthur said, his eyes opening. "No, I must face what I've done. It's not fair on Russell. I suppose I should explain myself, shouldn't I?"

"I know why you did it," Julia whispered, reaching out to touch his hand. "I understand."

Arthur smiled back, heartbreak obvious in every line on his face.

"If I could take it back, I would," Arthur explained. "I was a silly old man making a stupid mistake. I thought it would fix things, but I did the opposite. We're broken beyond repair. Before Simon came here, we were worried, but we weren't defeated. We would have found a way. We always did before. Simon came and ruined us. I shouldn't have been so short-sighted when thinking about the money, but I'm afraid one does get quite impatient when one gets to my age. Once you've seen it all, you think you know it all, but it turns out I still had much to learn. Simon was much worse than I think even you know. I couldn't believe the things Marvin told me. Do you know how he lost his last job?"

"No."

"Simon stole thousands from the club and framed Marvin," Arthur said with a sigh. "Simone Phoenix headlined their burlesque show, but the owners had offered to let Marvin co-headline as Tuna. They weren't even taking Simone off, they just wanted a new dynamic. Simon couldn't handle that, so he got rid of Marvin and he got away with it."

"That's awful."

"And it's only the start, poppet!" Arthur looked down at the picture again. "Poor Honey. Hhe already had it bad, but Simon was making things worse. He was demoralising and belittling the kid every chance he got. It started with the sly comments and names, but it got worse. Honey's costumes started going missing. It was pure bullying. I tried to have a word with Simon, but he called me a senile old codger! I even told him about Honey's mother, but he didn't care. I asked him why he was targeting Honey, and do you know what he said? 'Because I can'. That tore me up. In all my years, I've never known anyone so cruel. And it wasn't like Russell could do anything. Simon had him over a barrel. He was demanding money and threatening to ruin our reputation if he didn't get it. He was asking for thousands! And then there's the live singing. On the morning of that show, we had a drag family breakfast, like we always do. Simon announced that he was going to start singing live. When we were leaving, he looked me in the eye and said 'I guess we won't need you anymore'. That tore me up. I've given my heart and soul to this club. I've put in my years. Who was that man to hurt my family?

"I came back here and put the television on to calm down. There was a story on the local news about a man suing the council because a lamppost fell on him after a car hit it. He walked away with tens of thousands, and he wasn't even hurt! My mind instantly went to that new stupid rig. You know Simon didn't let us use it? It was only for his routine. He needed all those flashing lights and lasers to distract people from the fact he just wasn't very good.

"I didn't think about it, I just did it. I took one of Honey's saws from his toolbox and I waited. I almost backed out, but Simon started a row with Honey after he got off stage. I'd had enough. I thought if I injured Simon and we sued the lighting company, it was my way of killing two birds with one stone. I didn't realise how heavy that thing was. It should have killed him, but I didn't want it to. It took the whole song to cut through that thing, I almost thought it wasn't going to happen, and then it just snapped. I was horrified with myself. I ran back here. I didn't know what to do. I almost handed myself in right away, but I was scared. I got up early the next morning and hid the saw in the fish tank. It was silly, but I wasn't thinking straight. I didn't want to put it back in Honey's toolkit in case they connected it back to him. The longer I left it, the more it felt like my plan might work. Even up until tonight I had a glimmer of hope, even with the police sniffing around. I knew they had no real evidence, but when I found out they'd questioned Russell, I knew my time was up."

Arthur glanced at the clock on the mantelpiece

and stood up again.

"Speaking of which, this conversation has been on borrowed time," Arthur said as he looked around the flat with a downturned smile. "Will you finish packing up my photographs and give them to Honey? I want them to be a reminder to him that he can find family in many places. All I ever wanted to do was set an example for these kids. I regret to say that I've failed."

Arthur grabbed a coat from the hat stand and pulled it on. At that moment, sirens and blue flashing lights filled the courtyard.

"About time," Arthur announced with a nod. "I called them five minutes before you got here. I suppose this is a fitting end to a theatrical life. Who knows? I might even suit the prison uniform."

Julia held back tears as Arthur opened the door. Two uniformed officers walked towards him, one of them talking into a radio.

"I'm sorry, Arthur," Julia said, her tears no longer under control. "I'm so sorry."

"What for, poppet?" he said with a chuckle as he popped on a cream trilby hat. "I've had a fabulous life. This is merely the epilogue. The show must go on!

Remember that, Julia." Arthur paused and tapped his finger on his chin. "You know, you have a likeness of Hedy Lamarr."

With that, Arthur left the flat and walked towards the officers in the rain. After exchanging a few words, they attached a set of handcuffs and ducked him into the backseat of the police car. She stood in the doorway, tears streaming down her face as she watched them drive away. She stayed there long after the sirens were nothing more than an echo in her ear.

"The show must go on," she said to herself before turning back to the pictures to finish what Arthur had started.

CHAPTER 14

F ollowing Arthur's confession, they decided to stay in Blackpool for the remainder of their trip. Julia spent most of Thursday with Russell. She helped him with his tasks and provided a shoulder to cry on when he needed one. When Julia woke on Friday morning, she was less willing to say goodbye to Blackpool.

"Where's Jessie?" Julia asked Alfie when he

emerged from his room alone. "Don't tell me she's still asleep."

"She wasn't there when I woke up," Alfie said, pulling out his phone. "She sent me this text ten minutes ago telling us to meet her at the top of the tower in an hour."

"What is that girl up to?" Barker muttered as he dragged their cases from their room. "It's her birthday!"

They made their way down to the diner with their cases and had breakfast for the final time.

"What will happen to Arthur?" Alfie asked when he pushed his plate away. "It would be a shame if he spent the rest of his life behind bars."

"Depends if they go for grievous bodily harm or attempted murder," Barker said after sucking the air through his teeth. "It's hard to say, in this case. Even though Arthur didn't intend to kill Simon, it doesn't mean a court of law will believe him. It will all come down to witnesses and what Simon has to say. He could be the difference between life in prison and a couple of years."

"Let's hope he has a last-minute change of heart," Julia said after finishing her tea. "Stranger things have happened."

When Russell came over to take their plates away, he smiled at Julia, his eyes filled with sadness. The potential buyers for the B&B had put in an offer, which was currently sitting on his dressing table in the drag den. Julia had suggested he not rush into anything, but Russell insisted he had nothing left to give Sparkles by the Sea.

When it came time to check out, Julia was sad to leave Russell. Even though she had a conclusion to the mystery, she knew it had ripped Russell's life and soul apart.

"I'm sorry for everything," Julia said as she handed back the keys. "I wish I could have done more to help."

"You've done more than enough." Russell pulled her into a hug. "Don't feel sad, my Hedy Lamarr beauty queen. I'll find my way somehow. I always do."

As Julia pulled away from the hug, she hoped he would, even though she suspected he would never find happiness like he had known at Sparkles.

"If you're ever in the Cotswolds, I live in a beautiful village called Peridale," Julia said. "We even have a little B&B. It's not run by a drag queen, I'm afraid, but Evelyn is lovely."

"And nutty as a fruit cake," Barker added. "Good luck with everything."

Barker picked up their cases and set off towards the door with Alfie. Julia lingered by the fish tank desk, not wanting to leave her new friend like this. She hugged him again, squeezing him tightly.

"Go," Russell said with a smile when she finally pulled away. "They can't knock Lulu Suede down that easily. I'll be fine."

"Promise?"

"I promise."

Julia nodded, even if Russell's eyes told her something else. She turned on her heels and headed to the door, but she immediately stopped in her tracks when Barker opened the door to reveal Honey and what appeared to be an army of men behind him.

"What's this?" Russell called as Honey led the army into the hallway. "Where were you yesterday? I was trying to call you."

"Busy fixing everything," Honey said, planting his hands on his hips. "Recognise any of these faces? They're drag queens, Russell. Drag queens from all around Blackpool who know about this place's legacy and history and want it to continue. Drag queens, who out of the goodness of their own hearts, have agreed to become Sparkles Girls for free until this place is booming again."

"I – I don't understand," Russell said as he searched the faces. "Honey, it's too late."

"Have you signed the papers?"

"Well, no, but –"

"Then it's not too late," Honey cried, casting his hand back at the group of men. "For the sake of Arthur's legacy and for what he stood for, it's not too late. The world needs this place, and I'm willing to do whatever it takes to turn it around. This is my home. I don't have anything else."

At that moment, the sea of men parted, and Marvin walked through, a rucksack slung over his shoulder.

"I thought you'd gone to London?" Russell asked, his confusion deepening.

"I did," Marvin replied. "And the second I got off the train, I got on the next one right back because I knew I'd made a huge mistake leaving without telling you the truth."

"The truth?" Russell replied, gulping hard. "I don't think I can take any more truths this week."

Marvin took Russell's hand and led him into the drag den. He closed the door behind him, and they stayed in there for almost half an hour. The sea of drag queens moved into the bar area, leaving Julia, Barker, Alfie, and Honey to wait for them to emerge. When they did, Russell was holding a stack of papers in one hand, and Marvin's hand in the other. Both of them were smiling.

"This is madness," Russell said with a shake of his head as he dropped the paperwork on the counter. "You realise if I don't sign this, I'm throwing away hundreds of thousands of pounds for a gamble on a bunch of drag queens?"

"But if you do sign it," Honey said, sighing as he walked up to the counter, "what are you going to lose?"

Russell stared unblinkingly at Honey for what felt like a lifetime. He looked at Marvin, and then at Julia, and then at the contract. When he tore it in half, Julia's heart almost burst in her chest.

"I've lost the plot," Russell said as he tossed the two halves into a bin.

"You're a drag queen," Marvin said as he took Russell's hand again. "You never had it."

When Russell kissed Marvin, Julia decided it was time to go, and this time she was leaving without worry. She had a feeling Sparkles by the Sea would survive to entertain for another day.

"We're late to meet Jessie," Alfie said as he looked up at the tower. "Why do I feel like the surprises aren't over yet?"

They loaded their cases into the car once again and walked to the tower. After paying their admission fee, they travelled to the top floor of the building and waited for the lift. As they travelled the five hundred feet to the top, Julia's stomach flipped several times.

"Wow," she said as she looked at the view of the sea ahead when the lift doors opened. "Why didn't we come up here sooner?"

"I don't think she's here," Alfie said as he checked his phone. "I'll give her a call. I don't know what she thinks she's playing at."

Julia walked towards the edge of the observation tower where the floor and walls were made entirely of glass. She stepped onto the glass, the panel the only thing between her and the road below. The feeling was exhilarating, if not a little sickening. She looked ahead at the young woman in front of her who was standing right up to the edge of the glass, fearless of the dizzying drop below. When her phone started to ring, she pulled it out and turned around.

Julia stared at the fearless young woman, her heart dropping even further when she realised she was not a stranger at all, but someone very close to her.

"*Jessie?*" Julia cried. "Is that really you?"

Jessie's unruly dark hair had been cut up to her shoulders and shaped around her face with a full fringe resting against her eyebrows. Fiery red highlights had been added, giving it a sheen Julia had never seen from the teenager. Gone were the black hoody and baggy black jeans to be replaced with more fitted blue jeans, a white top, and a denim jacket. She was still wearing her clunky Doc Martens, but the restyle had transformed their look.

"Sis?" Alfie muttered, stepping forward, his phone still ringing in his hand. "What have you done?"

"Don't you like it?" she asked, self-consciously touching her new fringe.

"It's not that," Alfie replied, finally ending the

call. "You just look so – different. You look grown up."

Jessie smiled, her hair and clothes not the only thing different. Julia sensed a subtle shift in her mannerisms somehow. It was as though she had let something go.

"It's not so scary when you stand on it," Jessie said, turning and looking down at the ground. "It's actually quite soothing. It's a nice reminder that you can't fall if your feet are on solid ground." She turned back around and put her hands in her denim jacket. "I woke up with the sun this morning and walked back to Seabourne Avenue. It was almost like I was sleep walking, but something called me back there. When I realised where I was, I felt something click in me. Being here made me realise I've been holding onto so much anger for my whole life, and I don't need to anymore. I have everything I ever wanted. I'm happy."

"You look beautiful," Julia said. "Really beautiful."

"It's just new hair and new clothes," Jessie replied with a shrug. "But change is good, so why not make a complete change? I am eighteen now, after all. Can we go home now?"

"I'd like nothing more," Julia said as she wrapped her arm around Jessie's shoulder. "Happy birthday by the way."

"Thanks, Mum."

CHAPTER 15

Julia had to stop her foot from pressing down on the accelerator during the three-hour drive back home. When she saw the first sign for Peridale, she could not help but smile.

They pulled up outside the café, the 'Happy 18th Birthday Jessie!' banner hung up outside. Jessie blushed, but she smiled at the thought. Julia looked into the café, pleased that it was still standing, and glad that Katie had gathered everyone for the party like she had requested.

"Julia!" Katie squealed when she walked inside. "You're back! Oh, I must say, I'm quite sad to be leaving. I've had the time of my life! Where's Jessie?"

Julia looked around the café, her jaw dropping. Everything looked the same, except for the customers. At first, she thought Katie had filled the café with tanned strangers, until she realised they were the villagers.

"Do you like?" Katie exclaimed as she ran around the counter in her high heels, a frilly pink apron attached to her front. "I've sold out of the first batch already! I told you I'd have the whole village 'Glowing Like Katie'!"

"Did you have a lovely time in Blackpool?" Amy Clark asked as she sipped tea, the white china cup glowing against her neon orange face. "I wish I'd asked for an extra ticket for myself. I do love a good drag queen. Where's Jessie? Did you leave her behind?"

"I'm right here," Jessie said sheepishly. "Ta-da!"

A couple of the customers audibly gasped at Jessie's transformation, which caused her to blush even more.

"Jessie, you look so – *pale!*" Katie exclaimed as she ran around the counter to pull out a bottle of her tan. "We must change that right away!"

Over the next half an hour, they enjoyed tea and cake at the café while Jessie opened her cards and presents from the villagers and refused Katie's many offers of free bottles of tan. Just as they were about to leave to head home to unpack, Dot scurried across the village green, Barker's book clutched to her chest.

"Well, I say!" Dot exclaimed when she spotted Jessie. "Look at you! You look like a woman! Happy Birthday dear." Dot reached into her handbag and pulled out a stack of envelopes. "Don't use them all at once."

Jessie flicked through the envelopes, but it was obvious they were the vouchers Dot had won at the fête.

"You're looking better, Gran," Julia said with a smirk. "I hope you weren't sick for the whole week."

"Oh, I made that up, dear!" Dot exclaimed with a waft of her hand. "I wanted to stay home so I could read Barker's book in peace. I knew I wouldn't get a second to myself with all that sun and seagull squawking. I must say, Barker, you did a splendid job. It was like reading a real book!"

"It *is* a real book," he replied with a tight smile. "But from you, I'll take it. Thank you."

"I am a little upset that you included everyone else in the village and not me," Dot said with a sigh as she pushed up her curls at the back. "I kept waiting for my appearance, but I suppose you're saving that for the second book, right? A grand entrance in the first chapter as the new main character?"

Alfie whispered something in her ear before walking out of the café. As though she could sense the explosion, Jessie joined him.

"*Dora?*" Dot exclaimed. "I'm nothing like *Dora!* She's an interfering old nosey busy-body!"

Everyone in the café was suddenly distracted by their cups of tea. Deciding to leave Dot to vent, Julia climbed back into her car, and they drove up to her cottage. There was a yellow Mini parked in Julia's usual space. She parked behind it, curious as to whom the car belonged.

"Who's is that?" Jessie asked as she climbed out. "Are we expecting visitors?"

"It's yours," Barker said, patting Jessie on the

shoulder. "I bought it before we left for Blackpool and arranged for it to be dropped off."

"Are you serious?" Jessie cried, running over to the car. "You're not joking? This is really mine?"

"Cross my heart," Barker said with a chuckle. "It's not brand new, but it's only five years old and has only had one owner. It only has ten thousand miles on the clock and it's passed its MOT. Do you like it?"

Jessie ran around the car, her eyes widening with each step. Instead of replying, she ran to Barker and jumped on him, almost tackling him to the ground.

"I love it," she said, her eyes clenched as she hugged him tightly. "Can I take it out for a spin? Is it insured and taxed?"

"All sorted," Barker said as he patted her on the back. "They should have posted the keys through the letterbox, so she's all yours."

Jessie let go and ran for the door, pulling her house keys out of her pocket. She scooped them up and ran back to the car, her smile wider than Julia had ever seen it.

"You kept that quiet," Julia whispered to him. "It must have cost you a fortune."

"It's worth it," he whispered back as he wrapped his arm around Julia's shoulder. "Let's leave her to play with her new toy."

Julia unloaded the cases from the boot while Jessie and Alfie climbed into the front of the new car. With Barker's help, she carried them inside and put them in the hall. A stack of letters waited for her on the side table.

"You sort through those, and I'll put the kettle on," Barker said. "Peppermint and liquorice?"

"Yes, please," Julia said as she flicked through the various letters.

As she walked through to the sitting room, a large brown envelope caught her eye in the mass of junk mail and bills. She perched on the couch and ripped back the seal as Mowgli sauntered into the room. He jumped onto the chair arm and nudged her, but she was too distracted to stroke him. She stared at the certificate of adoption in her hands, Jessie's name in one box, Julia and Barker's in another. She looked at the envelope, the stamp dated the morning they had left for Blackpool.

"It's official," Julia said as she scooped Mowgli up. "We did it."

But as Julia stared at the certificate in her lap, she realised Arthur had been right when he had said it would not change a thing. She looked out the window and watched as Jessie set off down the lane in her new car. Julia felt as she had done for a long time, and the paper only served as an official confirmation. Jessie was her daughter, and nothing would ever change that.

When Barker entered with their cups, Julia accepted her comforting tea gratefully before passing him the certificate. As he read over the document, his lips following the words confirming that they were Jessie's legal guardians, Julia looked at her sparkling pearl engagement ring.

"How does an autumn wedding sound?" Julia asked as she held the ring up. "*This* autumn."

"Like the best idea you've ever had."

THANK YOU FOR READING & DON'T FORGET TO REVIEW!

I hope you all enjoyed taking a holiday with Julia and her family! Blackpool is one of my favourite places in the world, so I loved being able to take you along to experience a slice of the vibrant town.

If you did enjoy the book, **please consider** writing a review. They help us reach more people! I appreciate any feedback, no matter how long or short. It's a great way of letting other cozy mystery fans know what you thought about the book.

Being an independent author means this is my livelihood, and every review really does make a huge difference. Reviews are the best way to support me so I can continue doing what I love, which is bringing you, the readers, more fun adventures in Peridale! Thank you for spending time in Peridale, and I hope to see you again soon!

ALSO BY AGATHA FROST

The Scarlet Cove Series
Dead in the Water
Castle on the Hill
Stroke of Death

The Peridale Café Series
Pancakes and Corpses
Lemonade and Lies
Doughnuts and Deception
Chocolate Cake and Chaos
Shortbread and Sorrow
Espresso and Evil
Macarons and Mayhem
Fruit Cake and Fear
Birthday Cake and Bodies
Gingerbread and Ghosts
Cupcakes and Casualties
Blueberry Muffins and Misfortune
Ice Cream and Incidents

If you enjoyed *Blueberry Muffins and Misfortune*, why not sign up to Agatha Frost's **FREE** newsletter at **AgathaFrost.com** to hear about brand new releases!

You can also find Agatha on **FACEBOOK**, **TWITTER**, and **INSTAGRAM**. Simply search '**Agatha Frost**'.

The 14th book in the Peridale Café series is coming soon! Julia and friends will be back for another Peridale Cafe Mystery case later in the year.

11382323R00150

Printed in Germany
by Amazon Distribution
GmbH, Leipzig

BIGFOOT
AND
DOGMAN
SIGHTINGS
3